TRACEY WALSH

◆

TROUBLE IN
PARADISE

Complete and Unabridged

LINFORD
Leicester

First published in Great Britain in 2018

First Linford Edition
published 2020

A catalogue record for this book is available
from the British Library.

ISBN 978–1–4448–4400–9

Published by
F. A. Thorpe (Publishing)
Anstey, Leicestershire

Set by Words & Graphics Ltd.
Anstey, Leicestershire
Printed and bound in Great Britain by
T. J. International Ltd., Padstow, Cornwall

This book is printed on acid-free paper

Too Good to Be True?

Things were going great. Jenna had a great relationship, a great job, a great home. Great. It was when she found herself thinking that way that Jenna realised she had a problem.

Her life had been drifting along in a supposedly great way for months now and she knew sooner or later the chances were she was going to do something to ruin it — because she knew that drifting along wasn't in her nature. Something had to change.

'But I've never seen Shaun so happy,' Erica, Shaun's sister, said when she met Jenna for coffee.

'It's not him, it's me.' Jenna sighed. 'You'd think 'America's top teen agony aunt' would be so much better at relationships.' She gave a half smile to show Erica she was joking.

Jenna had been writing a problem

page for one of the top teen magazines for years. It was a job she'd fallen into when she won a writing contest when she was in high school. It didn't pay a fortune but it had helped her pay her way through college and still supplemented her meagre income from what she thought of as her proper writing.

As usual when her thoughts included financial matters, Jenna said a silent thank you for the safety net she kept in reserve.

'Well, Jenna, if you're sure you're happy with Shaun and you just want things to move on . . . '

'Yes,' Jenna interrupted, 'but I don't know how he feels. You know him better than anyone. What should I do?'

A few months earlier Jenna wouldn't have dreamed of confiding in Erica like this. The two women had clashed when Shaun had invited Jenna to move into the apartment he and his sister shared.

Jenna couldn't remember having done anything to cause Erica's hostility to her but from the first day Erica had done her best to make Jenna's life a misery.

Eventually Shaun had told his sister to either change her attitude or move out. The cold war that followed was barely more tolerable but they'd managed to live in the same space without killing each other which Jenna had supposed would have to do.

Then, just a few weeks ago, Erica's manner towards Jenna had changed. It was subtle at first — she'd offer to cook for all three of them or do more than her fair share of household chores. Without really noticing they had started to chat and socialise together. So when Erica made her next suggestion Jenna didn't find it too odd.

'I think you should propose.'

Jenna was silent for a moment as she pondered what her potential sister-in-law had just said.

'Seriously?' she said eventually.

Erica nodded.

'It's exactly what he needs. You know my brother. He doesn't know what he wants until someone hits him over the head with it.'

Jenna wasn't so sure but Erica's enthusiasm swept her along.

'Do it tonight,' Erica said. Jenna, Shaun and Erica were due to go to the big basketball final that night. A feeling that might have been excitement but was uncomfortably like nausea took over Jenna and she sat listening as Erica described how wonderful it would be when Shaun said yes and they all went out after the game to celebrate.

Jenna could see it too. It all sounded so easy. Maybe she should have looked a little closer at Erica as she talked away. Because a gleam had appeared in Erica's eye that looked awfully familiar. The way she used to look when she'd caused something to go wrong for Jenna in the early days.

The Wrong Answer

'Will you marry me?'

The next five seconds were the longest of Jenna's life. She was vaguely aware of her ear-to-ear grin sliding down her face. The look of pure horror on Shaun's face was the only response Jenna needed. She had her answer and she should have been able to pretend she was joking, laugh and move on.

A shame, then, that having listened to Erica she'd chosen to pop the question in front of thousands of people. Half time in the basketball game when the big screen showed what was going on in the crowd to fill in time before the teams came back on court.

The director had noticed Jenna doing the corny down-on-one-knee routine and had zoomed in. Shaun's obvious refusal was greeted at first by a stunned silence and then by jeers and chanting.

Mortified came nowhere near describing how Jenna felt. She didn't remember leaving her seat but she found herself heading to the exit, too stunned to cry.

She'd been so sure. After going over and over it with Erica she'd been so sure. So sure he'd say yes. Why wouldn't he? They'd been together for two years, shared an apartment for months. They might as well have been married.

Although it wasn't something Jenna would have thought of herself in a million years, once Erica had talked her into it the basketball final had seemed the ideal venue for a proposal.

Now, as she trudged home through the rain soaked streets, it started to sink in just how cringe-worthy her situation was. Any faint hope she might have had that the episode would be quickly forgotten was dashed when her phone started pinging with social media notifications.

Reaching it from her pocket she soon

realised things were worse than she'd thought. Someone had uploaded the big screen video and it showed every sign of going viral.

As she neared home it dawned on Jenna what she had to do. She had an hour, max, before Shaun would be following her home. It crossed her mind briefly that he might leave the game early under the circumstances but that was never going to happen.

Jenna gave herself 45 minutes to pack a bag and get out of there. She could pick up the rest of her stuff when the dust had settled but her priority was to get as far away as she could as fast as she could.

Boring considerations like work and responsibilities — none of that stuff was on her radar at that moment. The trauma she'd just gone through had pretty much given her a personality transplant. Every single part of her was focused on one thing — getting away right now.

Jenna would've liked to be one of

those women who, in this situation, would pack a bag and jump on the first flight available, wherever that may be. But her fear of flying seemed to be the only part of her personality that was still intact.

So, once her trolley case was packed and she'd done a sweep of the apartment to make sure she had all her essentials, Jenna prepared to leave for the train station.

She had a vague idea of how to get to her chosen destination and even if she had to spend the night in the station it would be preferable to being in the apartment when Shaun arrived home.

A few taps of an app showed Jenna she could travel through the night and a long train ride and short bus ride later she should reach her destination after a ridiculous number of hours compared to a quick flight. The train fare was extortionate, though, and she had to make a quick dash to the ATM.

Subconsciously she must have been covering her tracks already, not wanting to pay by card. Her phone was driving her mad, clocking up the notifications of all the shared posts cataloguing her embarrassment.

In another totally out of character moment Jenna dumped her beloved phone in the next waste bin she passed, then headed into the station, her coat hood shielding her from the CCTV cameras at the entrance.

Jenna didn't know why her 'fight or flight' instinct compelled her to run, or why she thought the setting of her idyllic childhood holidays was the place to run to. But a little voice told her, 'Jenna, you're doing exactly the right thing.'

Note to self: Jenna — if you'd known what a lot of trouble it would cause, you might be tempted to ignore that little voice next time . . .

Warning Bells

The bus journey from Tampa across the Sunshine Skyway bridge brought Jenna back to life. The exhaustion of the endless hours on the train melted away and she looked around her with the same enthusiasm she used to feel when her family crossed this bridge to start their vacations.

For so many years she'd lost count, they'd gone to St Pete Beach for the whole month of August. It wasn't just the highlight of her year but the highlight of her entire childhood and early teenage years.

Memories of her parents threatened to dampen her mood so she forced herself to look ahead. Could she dare to hope that Alex might still be here?

Alex had lived at the hotel where they stayed every year. Jenna couldn't remember whether his father owned it or was just a live-in manager. She guessed the family must have owned the place as their large brood of kids overran the hotel at times.

Alex was the oldest of seven brothers and a sister. Jenna tried to remember their names — the little girl, Amber, was easiest. Then there were six boys whose names also began with the letter A. Alan? Andy? Jenna was just guessing.

Alex had to help out around the place too as he got older but whenever he could he came to find Jenna and they spent magical hours together.

'I'm going to marry you one day, Jenna,' Alex had said one day when they were both about twelve. Jenna giggled but her heart felt as if it would burst.

'You promise?' she said.

This memory placed a warm smile on Jenna's face. Neither of them would have talked that way to any of the kids they knew at school. It was as if they squeezed all their feelings into that one month a year. And, strangely, they never

11

kept in touch during the rest of the year.

When Jenna's family left the hotel she would say goodbye to Alex with a hug and a tacit understanding that romance was on hold until the following summer.

Then when Jenna was sixteen her parents died in an accident and she hadn't seen Alex since.

The bus drew up at her stop and Jenna lugged her case down. She could hardly believe she was standing in front of a place that held so many memories.

She didn't have long to wait to find out whether Alex was still there. As she entered the reception area her eyes were drawn to a man standing with his back to her, hammering a picture hook into the wall. It was unmistakably Alex and Jenna's heart did a roller-coaster swoop that had never once happened with Shaun.

In that moment Jenna realised something. After the fiasco of the proposal she'd thought that her overriding feeling was of humiliation.

But now she knew that mixed in with it was another feeling. Relief. She was glad Shaun had turned her down. And standing here a few feet from the real love of her life, that relief was growing.

Jenna took a deep breath and was seconds away from calling Alex's name when a beautiful black-haired woman entered the reception office and took the words right out of her mouth.

'Alex, I'm back.'

'Hey.' Alex turned and bestowed a breathtaking smile on the woman. Then he spotted Jenna and the smile turned to a stunned expression. 'Jenna?' he said.

'You're Jenna?' The scornful tone the woman used to ask this brought a flush to Jenna's cheeks as she realised what a state she must look after her long journey.

Her next thought was one of pleasure as she realised Alex must have talked to this woman about her even though it was years since they'd lost touch.

But the hopeful pang in her heart was quickly replaced by disappointment as she realised that the two people before her were obviously close.

'Yes,' she said. 'I was in the neighbourhood and I thought I'd stop by and say hi.'

Pathetic, she thought. But Alex didn't seem to find the idea so strange.

'It's so great to see you,' he said, striding towards her and wrapping his arms around her in a suffocating bear hug.

The other woman's face took on a steely look as she cleared her throat to remind them she was there.

'Oh, I'm sorry. Jenna, this is Christina. Her dad owns the place now.' Hmm, Jenna thought. Daddy owns the hotel, Christina owns Alex by the look of things. 'How long are you in town for?'

'I'm not sure. I thought I might treat myself to a few nights here and then maybe look for somewhere cheaper to stay for a while.' Jenna could read Christina's thoughts — didn't sound much like someone who was just in the neighbourhood, did it?

The phone in the office rang and Christina reluctantly went to answer it. Alex picked up Jenna's case and they walked towards the guest huts that faced on to the beach.

As a kid Jenna had fantasised about staying in one of the huts but for some reason her mother had always preferred to stay in the accommodation at the back of the hotel.

'We have a couple of huts available. Let's leave your stuff in this one and then we can have a drink and catch up,' Alex said.

Things were moving a little more quickly than Jenna was comfortable with but she took a deep breath and followed him.

Ten minutes later they were sitting at the bar looking out to sea and sipping beers. If Jenna had been letting her imagination carry her away, Alex's next words brought her down to earth with a bump.

'Jenna, it's so great to see you but I have to tell you — Christina's my girlfriend. I'm not saying I thought you'd come here to try and rekindle some sort of great romance or anything, I just thought you should know.'

Hoping the disappointment didn't show on her face Jenna nodded.

'Don't be silly. I just wanted to look up an old friend. I hope we can still say we're friends?'

They chatted for an hour or so, comparing notes about how life had treated them since they last saw each other. Alex already knew the reason Jenna hadn't been back to Florida. Her parents had died there, after all.

Time had allowed Jenna to pretend she'd come to terms with it but it was still a mystery. Why had they rushed down to Florida without her, telling her they'd only be gone for a few days and she couldn't miss school?

She'd stayed with her best friend's

family while they were gone and it was those kind people who had taken her in so she could finish school. The alternative would have been moving across the country to live with her uncle and his family.

As for Alex, his main concern was how boring he must seem, having stayed in the same place he'd lived all his life.

'When Dad got ill and the hospital bills needed paying, he and Mom had no choice but to sell this place,' he explained. 'The rest of the family live in town now and I work two jobs to help out. I could probably make more if I moved somewhere bigger but . . . '

'But if you live in paradise why would you want to leave?' Jenna said and their eyes met.

Alex's smile spoke more than words. He wasn't used to people understanding that. Christina was always dropping hints about moving to live in the city. It was the main reason he hadn't felt ready to move their relationship on to a

17

more serious level.

Just at that moment, Christina appeared in the doorway.

'Alex, the head of maintenance is looking for you,' she said. 'Just because your childhood sweetheart's turned up doesn't mean you can take the day off.' She was smiling but it was a smile that hadn't reached as far as her eyes.

'I'll see you later, Jenna,' Alex said and hurried off to find his colleague.

Christina climbed on to the bar stool he'd vacated and signalled for a drink. The two women looked out to sea in silence for a few minutes and Jenna wondered if she should try to come up with a safe subject to talk about. But it was clear Christina wanted to be in charge of this exchange.

'Alex is happy,' she said. 'You can see that just by looking at him. It hasn't always been that way. Apparently some girl screwed up his life by walking away and never looking back.'

It took Jenna a moment to realise what Christina was getting at.

'He was damaged goods when I came along. Took me a while to get through to him. But now? We're good together. So, you know, back off — OK?' With that she left her hardly touched drink on the bar and stalked back to her office.

Jenna was shocked. Within the space of a couple of hours she had gone from hopeful traveller to reunited friend. Now she was being warned off by a woman she barely knew.

Was her decision to come here a stupid one? Maybe she should have holed up in some anonymous town she'd never been to before.

After having a quick meal in the hotel restaurant, Jenna went back to her guest hut and signed on to her laptop. If there was one thing she was still in control of it was her work. She checked her e-mails (nothing from Shaun or Erica, what a surprise) and then signed into the system that allowed her to write her 'Ask Jenna' column.

There were usually a fair number of

messages each day and Jenna would select a few to answer in the column. Whichever she thought was the best question would be featured as the star query and Jenna's deadline for choosing one was the next day.

She scrolled through lots of boring, unoriginal stuff before marking a couple that were more interesting. Then she stopped with a jolt. The most recent message might have been a candidate for star of the week if it hadn't been so sinister.

'Dear Jenna,' it said. ''I don't know what to do. I plucked up the courage to tell my boyfriend I wanted to move our relationship on to something more serious. In fact I proposed to him.

'But when I asked him to marry me he just laughed. And what's worse, I asked him in front of all our friends and now I never want to see any of them again. What would you do? Love from Nonnie.'

Mixed Emotions

First thing next morning Jenna went for a walk to clear her head. The strange Ask Jenna e-mail that seemed to echo her own recent experience was preying on her mind.

Within a few minutes she'd decided the e-mail was just a coincidence. She also made the decision not to include it in this week's magazine column. Jenna could hardly advise anyone in a similar situation to run away the length of the country from the problem.

Jenna had chosen three questions to answer this week already and she usually sent in three or four, so her editor would be happy with that.

She pondered the three questions, coming up with quirky but helpful answers in her head as she walked. All she would need to do when she got back was quickly type them up and e-mail them.

Jenna thought for about the millionth time since she'd landed the magazine job how lucky she was. She enjoyed her Ask Jenna role but it was hardly demanding and it left her with plenty of free time to concentrate on what she thought of as her serious writing. She had a list as long as her arm of articles she wanted to write and one day she'd pursue her dream of finishing her first novel.

It was one of Jenna's recurring nightmares that the editor of *Like!* magazine would decide they needed someone younger for the column. And it wasn't the money it brought in, but rather the feeling that, even though she found it easy, she was helping young people who were going through some really tough times.

She'd lost count of the number of girls who'd written back months later to tell her how things had worked out after they followed her advice. They always said how lucky they felt to have found someone to confide in, even if that someone was just a page in a magazine. That word 'lucky' again.

Of course, the factor that allowed Jenna to live off her part-time income wasn't quite so lucky. When she'd lost her parents at such a young age she'd been devastated but, financially at least, her future had been taken care of.

At the time her uncle, who dealt with her parents' estates, had tried to explain to her the ins and outs of trust funds and investments but all she'd taken in was that she wouldn't need to worry about money as long as she was sensible.

Jenna was shaken from her morose thoughts by the sight of a familiar figure up ahead on the beach. Alex hadn't seen her approaching so she stood and watched him for a few moments.

Alex seemed to have been frozen in time since the last time she saw him down here when they were teenagers. Dressed in cargo shorts, his yellow T-shirt discarded on the sand, he was laying out sets of scuba diving equipment.

Intrigued, Jenna moved forward and it was only then she saw a group of young people also paying close attention to Alex.

Jenna stopped in her tracks and watched this happy, confident Alex instructing his audience. When she'd seen Alex at the hotel the previous day Jenna had been struck by how passive he seemed to be in Christina's presence. She was relieved now to see the Alex she remembered.

Reluctant to distract him, she backtracked along the beach and saw a hut she'd previously ignored. The sign on the hut said simply 'St Pete Diving School' and it was only when she came up close she saw the smaller wording that explained what she'd just seen. Alex ran the diving school as well as working for Christina's father at the hotel.

That explained the two jobs he'd mentioned. It was typical of Alex to be modest and not to bother mentioning that his second job was actually a business he'd set up himself.

Jenna was impressed. She knew Alex's family weren't well off any more so he must have built this up from scratch. Jenna tried to convince herself that her feelings were simply pleasure at an old friend's success but she knew deep down she was in danger of being overwhelmed by old emotions and the remembrance of unfulfilled dreams.

For years she'd kept thoughts of Alex buried as she got on with her life but she was starting to realise her feelings for him had never disappeared; those feelings must have been buried deep while she tried to build a relationship with Shaun but now they were rising to the surface.

* * *

Jenna returned to her hotel room determined to keep control of her re-emerging emotions. She went back to her laptop to type up her Ask Jenna answers and after sending her article to her editor she ran through her other e-mails to do some deleting and organising as she always did after completing her weekly column.

At first Jenna couldn't work out what was odd about what she was seeing. Then it hit her. The odd question that had been there earlier — the one that seemed to mirror her own experience — had gone. She checked her deleted messages to see if she'd inadvertently deleted it but it wasn't there.

Jenna sat staring at her screen for a while, unable to work out what had happened. In the end she decided, as she was by no means an IT expert, to forget about it. It was probably some sort of bug in the software.

Disturbing Memories

'Hey, Jenna!'

Jenna smiled as she turned to see Alex striding towards her. She'd been about to set off on yet another walk, after spending most of the day glued to her laptop searching for available properties nearby. She'd hardly noticed the day slipping away.

Now she realised walking on the beach was the only way she could relax and take her mind off the crazy situation she'd left behind in New York.

'Hi, Alex,' she said and as he stopped next to her they both hesitated for a second before he gave her a kiss on the cheek and they hugged.

'Where d'you think you're going, alone in the dark?' Alex said. 'It's not as safe round here as it used to be when we were kids, you know.'

It wasn't actually dark yet, though

27

the sun was starting to fade. Jenna felt silly for deciding to set out at this time. But after gazing at the sea from the decking outside her guest hut for several minutes she'd been unable to resist.

'Don't suppose you fancy coming with me?' she asked. 'Just a quick walk down the beach to stretch my legs.' Jenna knew she was playing with fire but almost managed to convince herself it was an innocent suggestion.

Alex glanced at his watch and then back at the hotel before answering.

'Sure. I have to be back soon, though.'

Jenna smiled but she was thinking about the hold Christina must have over Alex, if going for a walk with an old friend was such a tough decision. She decided not to beat about the bush.

'Christina seems . . . confident,' she said as they set off along the boardwalk that led to the beach.

Alex didn't answer. He stared out towards the sea with a look on his face that Jenna couldn't decipher. Instantly she felt guilty, without even knowing why, although her words did seem to have been a veiled criticism of Alex's girlfriend.

It was unfair of her to turn up out of the blue and start commenting on someone she didn't even know.

'All this walking is helping me to unwind after that awful train journey down here.' The complete change of subject brought a frown to Alex's face but then he caught on to Jenna's desire to steer conversation away from Christina.

'Are you going to tell me why you left New York?' he asked.

Jenna had managed to avoid the subject until now but she realised being able to talk about it might help. She'd always been able to talk to Alex and she had no reason to think that might have changed.

Jenna gave him a brief rundown of the proposal rejection and braced herself for his reaction. She was actually surprised the online video hadn't reached him on social media, though having said that, Alex was one of the few people she knew who didn't spend all their time glued to their phones.

The thought of a phone reminded Jenna she still needed to set up the phone she'd picked up in Tampa. Once she'd finished giving him the edited highlights of her humiliation Alex reacted exactly as she'd hoped he would. Instead of laughing or making light of the situation he was sympathetic.

'You poor thing,' he said, wrapping his strong arms around her and enveloping her in a comforting bear hug. The feel and scent of him so close started Jenna's emotions going haywire.

He was at once familiar and yet a completely different person to the young man she had known before. One thing was certain. However much Jenna had tried to convince herself over the years that their relationship had been nothing more than a recurring holiday romance, she knew now that it was real. But was she reading too much into Alex's kindness and sympathy? There was only one way to find out.

Jenna raised her head until she was staring straight into Alex's blue eyes. Closing her own eyes she placed a gentle kiss on his lips and waited for his response.

She didn't have to wait long. Alex pushed her away so strongly that she almost stumbled backwards on to the sand.

'What are you doing?' he shouted.

'I'm sorry,' Jenna said. 'It just felt so right.' Then she turned and ran back to her room, flung herself on the bed and waited for the tears to start. Surprisingly she remained dry-eyed, as if her system couldn't cope with any more emotional outbursts after her recent experiences. A few minutes later she heard a knock on the door.

'Jenna, let me in,' Alex said softly through the door. 'We need to talk.'

Actually, that's the last thing I need

at this precise moment, Jenna thought, reluctantly dragging herself from the bed. She opened the door but stood in the way so Alex couldn't come in. If she was going to be humiliated again she wanted to have the option of closing the door whenever she chose.

'Jenna, I'm sorry I reacted that way,' Alex said. 'You took me by surprise, that's all.'

'No, it was wrong of me,' Jenna said. 'I know you're with Christina. I shouldn't have kissed you. I'm just so confused at the moment — it's like I don't know what I'm doing half the time.'

Alex looked at her in silence for what seemed like hours but was actually just a few seconds.

'It's not as if I'm not flattered,' he said. Jenna was about to shout at him for that comment but then she saw the grin slowly appearing on his face. He'd always known how to wind her up. Whatever — he was trying to make light of it and Jenna was relieved.

She gave him a playful cuff over the head. Alex turned to go and Jenna watched him until he disappeared into the darkness at the other side of the path.

How different might life have been, Jenna wondered, if it weren't for that tragic accident that had taken her parents away from her? Would she and Alex have continued to see each other every year and would that have developed into something more permanent? Obviously she could never know.

Jenna was too wound up to sleep so she thought she might as well type up some of her thoughts in her journal and then get a head start on her next column.

Often the editor would pass on questions to her via e-mail as they arrived so she signed on to her laptop to see if any had appeared.

There was just one: 'Dear Jenna, I'm finding it hard to cope with the death of my parents. They both died suddenly in a car accident and I feel guilty because

I wasn't with them. Now I have to go and live with strangers until I'm old enough to look after myself. How will I survive?'

The letter, like many she received, was anonymous. And like the one that had mysteriously disappeared earlier, this 'problem' was spookily like Jenna's own experience. An experience she had, just a few minutes ago, been writing about in her journal. Once she could put down to coincidence, but twice within days?

Jenna was starting to get the feeling someone was targeting her. She copied the e-mail in case it disappeared like the last one. She wasn't sure why but she wanted to make sure she had evidence. She'd sound crazy if she tried to explain this to her editor or anyone else.

It took her a long time to drift off to sleep that night. The strange e-mails had triggered memories she'd tried to suppress for years.

It was natural that being here in Florida would bring back memories of her happy childhood holidays with her parents but the words in that e-mail had been almost a copy of her journal entry and had opened up a whole other level of memories that weren't so good.

For months after she'd lost her parents she'd felt the weight of an unbearable guilt. It was the only time they'd gone to Florida without her and they'd never returned. Her teenage logic made it her fault they'd died.

If she'd been with them maybe they wouldn't have hired that particular car, or maybe they wouldn't have been on that road at that time. She ignored the fact that it hadn't been her choice to stay behind.

The family she was living with could do little but watch as she shrank away from the world. Eventually they contacted her uncle and he arranged for Jenna to have some counselling.

She'd been sceptical about it but after a few months she felt herself escaping from the depths of despair and starting to enjoy life again. The experience had made her an advocate for grief counselling and she still had sessions occasionally even now.

The main benefit of the counselling had been to work on those guilt feelings that had swamped her. They'd never gone away completely but most of the time she could rationalise what had happened and tell herself she hadn't been in control of any of it.

So how come a weird e-mail arriving out of the blue had the power to dredge it all up again? And not only that. How had the sender of the e-mail managed to echo the thoughts she herself had been having just minutes earlier?

The fact that she had been writing about her memories shortly before the e-mail arrived had really disturbed Jenna but she knew she had to try and put it out of her mind and get some rest.

At last she drifted off to sleep and although she had feared the mixture of emotions would lead to nightmares, instead she enjoyed a night's deep, untroubled sleep.

Next morning she headed to the hotel's beach bar for breakfast. This had always been Jenna's favourite place to eat when they holidayed here and she breathed in the rich scent of Colombian coffee as she sat waiting for her food.

The beach was fairly quiet at this time and it was definitely the part of the day Jenna enjoyed most. A shame, then, that her enjoyment was about to be interrupted.

Jenna heard Christina before she saw her and then all at once she was standing beside Jenna's table.

'Still here?' Christina said.

Jenna resisted the temptation to make a facetious remark about stating the obvious.

'For a couple more days, yes,' she said. 'I have a list of rental properties to look at before I choose one.'

Christina's eyes narrowed. The news that Jenna was still planning to stay in the area obviously hadn't pleased her. Without another word she stalked away.

Determined not to let Christina's attitude put her off her breakfast, Jenna tucked into the loaded plate that had just been delivered to her table. Ouch, too hot, she thought and powered up her laptop while she waited for the food to cool.

She opened the page with the property details, surprising herself by feeling grateful to Christina for jogging her memory.

By the time she'd finished eating, Jenna had arranged to meet an agent to view three of the properties but she'd already set her heart on one of them.

Halfway between the hotel and the centre of town, with an enviable beachfront position, the small house looked perfect for her. And even better, it was available on a short-term lease so she could move on as soon as she got itchy feet again, if she ever did.

Jenna had only been back in the area for a matter of hours and yet she felt a sense of belonging. It wasn't just her

feelings for Alex that had been reawak-
ened but memories of a place she had
loved. Although she had only spent
holidays here it felt like home, somehow.

Jenna briefly thought about Shaun.
Should she have got in touch with him
to let him know she was all right? She
only wondered for a moment, then the
way she'd felt at the game came back to
her.

She doubted if he'd worried about
her for more than a minute once he
realised she'd left. He was probably out
drinking with his mates the next night
as if nothing had happened.

Then another thought crept in. All
his mates and all their friends would
have seen the video of her being
humiliated. Every time she thought
about it she felt sick and after the huge
breakfast she'd just put away that was
not a good idea.

Jenna resolved to put thoughts of
Shaun and the proposal firmly to the
back of her mind for now. She had

wasted enough hours on the journey down here dissecting their relationship and the only conclusion she'd been able to reach was that they should never have got together in the first place. She had to acknowledge, on her part at least, it had been a case of settling for someone through a fear of being alone.

Ever since her parents' deaths when she was sixteen Jenna had had a fear of being alone and would do almost anything to ensure she didn't find herself having to put up with her own company.

She envied people who enjoyed solitude. So that's how she'd ended up moving in with Shaun even though Erica had done everything in her power to stop it happening.

That really wasn't a good basis for a relationship, she now realised. Jenna's determination to find somewhere to stay was combined with a resolve to become more comfortable living alone.

She gathered up all her things and headed back to her room to get ready for her property viewing trip. She didn't notice Christina watching her from outside the beach bar, where she'd been standing the whole time, watching her eat.

When Jenna left her room and walked to the hotel entrance, Christina slipped into the room using her pass key.

Where the Heart Is

The first house Jenna viewed left her feeling as if her hurried decision to stay here was a mistake. The online details had described it as having a beach location. Yes, if you stood on the kitchen work top and pressed your face to the window you could just see a sliver of sand and possibly a hint of the sun shining on the sea.

Apart from that, the whole place needed refurbishment and as she'd be renting that would be down to the landlord. It looked as if it was last decorated in the 80s so she didn't imagine the landlord put this place at the top of their priority list.

The agent who had picked her up at the hotel and was accompanying her on the viewings was most apologetic.

The second house made up for it, however. This was the one Jenna had already decided would be the best and it was perfect. A pale blue wooden clapboard structure, it was situated within a few yards of the beach and had its own pathway down to the sand.

Jenna could imagine waking each morning and taking her coffee out on to the decking that looked out to sea.

It would make a great writing retreat and yet it was also a welcoming place that felt perfect for building new friendships. It was about a mile from the hotel and the same distance from the centre of town.

Currently without transport, that suited Jenna as she'd be able to walk into town easily. She made a mental note to start looking for a car soon.

As for the hotel, she would need to put it, and Alex, out of her head for now. On top of everything else that had happened lately, her feelings for Alex were just too confusing. He and Christina were obviously committed to each other and it wouldn't be fair for her to try to come between them.

The agent's phone buzzed and she excused herself to go outside and answer the call. Jenna was relieved as it gave her the chance to wander around the whole of the building on her own for a few minutes.

The top floor was taken up by the large master bedroom and en-suite plus a small spare room. A large window at one end of the master bedroom looked out on to the beach. The only problem with this house, Jenna realised, would be how to drag herself away from that view.

Downstairs there was a cosy sitting-room and a kitchen/dining-room that again looked out over the sea. The kitchen was on the small side but that didn't bother Jenna too much. She'd never been much of a cook and she didn't plan to start now. Over recent years she'd become expert at living on a diet of salads, sandwiches and take-aways.

Maybe that was why Shaun had looked so appalled at the idea of marrying her, she thought. Then she smiled as she realised it was the first time she'd been about to think about that awful moment with a touch of humour.

Maybe she was going to survive the humiliation after all. And maybe this house was somewhere she could enjoy being alone at last.

In her mind's eye Jenna could already see herself living happily here. She could picture the furniture she'd choose for each room and yet again she felt grateful knowing she had enough money in the bank to pay for it all.

She was starting from scratch and would need everything from bedroom furniture right down to plates and cutlery. She felt a small glow of excitement rising within her and then instantly felt ridiculous for being excited by such a thing.

It crossed Jenna's mind to cancel the third house viewing she'd arranged, but the agent was persuasive. Probably being paid per viewing, she thought.

At least the third house proved to her how special the second one had been. This one was tiny and although Jenna didn't need a huge amount of space she didn't like the idea of rooms so small that you could almost touch each wall as you stood in the centre.

'Can we go back to the last place?' she asked, and the agent smiled. Within the hour Jenna had signed up and arranged to move in. She'd need to stay at the hotel for a couple more nights but at least things were in motion. She could spend the days in between searching for a car and ordering furniture for her new house.

'So how long do you think you'll be staying in the area?' the agent had asked while they were sorting out the paperwork. Jenna had signed a six-month lease but she appreciated the attempt at small talk.

'I'm not sure,' she said. 'I might decide to put down roots permanently.' The words were out before Jenna had even registered the thought. It was true, though.

Something about the area, and the house, felt like home. That feeling she had noticed since arriving back here was growing stronger all the time.

Prying Eyes

While Jenna was out on her house-hunting trip, Christina carefully searched through her belongings in the guest hut. Not much with her, she thought with a sigh of relief. Does that mean she won't be around long?

Outwardly, Christina came across as super confident and assured. Only she knew how fragile her outer shell could be. Nobody was allowed to see the insecure, anxious inner self she hid deep inside.

Even her close family — or even Alex — would have said she was the toughest person they knew. But right now that outer shell was close to cracking — and all because of Jenna Logan.

That moment the other day when the strange young woman had appeared in reception looking for Alex was indelibly printed on Christina's brain. The look on his face as he stared at her betrayed feelings he'd never shown to Christina. Oh, and it was mutual, that much was obvious.

When Christina realised this, it triggered feelings that surprised her. Throughout her relationship with Alex Shepherd she had always felt like she was the one in charge.

As if all she had to do was ask and Alex would do anything for her. But she'd never seen that look in his eyes when he looked at her. It hurt, like her heart was being pierced. Christina wasn't used to being made to feel second best and she didn't like it one bit.

She slowly looked through Jenna's belongings with a critical eye. The clothes were obviously chosen more for comfort than style.

Christina's own wardrobe, heavily subsidised by her father, was dominated by designer labels and up-to-the-minute fashion trends. Whatever it was that Alex saw in Jenna it certainly wasn't her dress sense. No, their mutual attraction was rooted in something Christina couldn't compete with.

Years of childhood and teenage friendship were something that couldn't be wiped away. And the thing that was starting to eat away at Christina was that she didn't know the extent of that friendship, or relationship.

Friendship. That had always been an alien word to Christina. Thinking back to her high-school days was like pressing on a bruise to see if it still hurt.

Her family had moved around like nomads during those years and usually Christina blamed that for the miserable time she'd had. Her father worked for one of the most famous hotel chains in the country and his speciality was being brought into failing hotels and turning their fortunes round.

He and Christina's mother both believed that families belonged together so they would have to move when he did. It was probably the only thing her parents had agreed on.

Christina was an only child and had always been Daddy's little princess. He was the fun parent while Mom took on the role of disciplinarian. When the stress of moving once too often led to Christina's mother admitting defeat and asking for a divorce, it was natural that Christina would opt to stay with her dad.

Living in the staff quarters of various luxury hotels, Christina's life outside school was great fun and quite glamorous. She grew used to bumping into famous actors and musicians and whenever she managed to make a friend they would be star struck.

But friends were few and far between and Christina hated school with a passion. She always seemed to be the new girl — she and her dad rarely stayed in one place longer than six months.

Each time she started at a new high school Christina tried to see it as an opportunity for a fresh start. She was bright, academically, and never had any trouble catching up with what was being studied in her classes. It was the social side that was the problem.

It was as if she had a target painted on her back inviting the latest set of mean girls to zero in on her. Within days she would become aware of spiteful rumours being spread about her or conversations coming to an abrupt end when she walked by.

Eventually Christina started to grow the hard exterior shell she still presented to the world. Those lonely years had made her the woman she was now. And yet if you asked most people who knew her now, they wouldn't have a clue about any of that.

Her father had been unaware of it at the time and Christina would rather walk on hot coals than admit she'd been bothered by how she was treated by school bullies.

She was proud of herself for surviving those years and it was only at very dark times that she thought back to those days. What Christina didn't realise or acknowledge was that denying the effect experiences have had doesn't erase them.

It was only recently, since her relationship with Alex had become serious, that Christina had fully under-stood how lonely she had been. Now the girlfriends of Alex's friends had started to include her in their crowd and she'd slowly started to open herself up to their friendship.

And now, faced with overwhelming feelings of insecurity regarding Alex and Jenna, the same kind of survival instinct as she'd felt years ago was starting to emerge.

It wouldn't only be Alex she lost to Jenna if her worst fears came true, it would be her whole new social life. She couldn't bear the idea of returning to those friendless times.

Christina's thoughts started to race. The irresistible urge that had forced her to sneak into Jenna's room still wasn't satisfied. She looked around for something she could take her jealous feelings out on.

There was a framed photo on the bedside table. Two adults and a young girl on a beach. Not unlike some of the family snaps she herself treasured. It would be too obvious if she took or damaged it. There had to be something else.

Christina's attentions switched to the small desk near the window. Jenna's laptop sat open and the power light was on. Christina touched the space bar on the keyboard and the screen came to life. Jenna must be very trusting — the last document she'd worked on was displayed. No password request or anything.

Christina skimmed through the document. Her hands were itching to delete everything from the computer and wreck Jenna's work but again that would be too obvious. Jenna would surely suspect someone had been in the room and deliberately sabotaged her laptop.

No, she had to be patient. She'd find a way to get at Jenna that would be more subtle. And more effective. Something that would make Jenna Logan leave town for good.

Glancing at her watch, Christina realised she'd been in Jenna's room far longer than she'd planned. That was what always seemed to happen when she slipped back into thoughts of the past. Time would run away with her and she'd find it hard to come back to reality.

But this time was different. She felt refreshed, as if she'd awoken from a deep sleep with her thoughts and objectives organised and clear. Daddy always said she was a great planner. Well, her new project would put that to the test.

Christina was torn between two desires. The first, and most urgent, was to get rid of Jenna and get her life back to normal. Everything had been fine until Jenna showed up.

Alex was as devoted to Christina as a

puppy and the way things had been going she was sure it wouldn't have been long before he asked her to marry him.

They'd been together such a long time it was starting to become embarrassing when people asked her when they were getting married.

But she'd heard that Jenna was looking for somewhere to stay nearby more permanently. If that happened then Christina's second desire would come into play. She wanted to hurt Jenna. Hurt her so much that staying around here would not be an option.

Alarming Reaction

By the time Jenna returned to the hotel she was buzzing with the excitement of having found her new house. She hesitated to call it a home because she had no idea how long she'd be living there.

Home implied being settled as far as Jenna was concerned and although there had been plenty of places she'd enjoyed living she didn't really consider that she'd had a home since she had to leave the one she shared with her parents.

Her most recent living arrangements, sharing with Shaun and Erica, had been fun for the most part. But she wouldn't want to relive the months before Erica had finally accepted her.

Letting herself into the guest hut Jenna hesitated on the threshold. Something felt odd but she couldn't put her finger on it. Then it registered. There was a faint hint of perfume and it was vaguely familiar.

Jenna herself didn't bother with expensive fragrances. A quick burst of whichever body spray she'd grabbed when shopping was enough for her. But this was different. A heavy, heady smell of flowers and sweet, almost sickly spices.

She'd smelled it before and it was a moment before she realised when. It was the previous day when Christina had joined her at the bar. Jenna remembered the overpowering perfume that hung over them both when they talked.

Of course, it wasn't that surprising that Christina should have been in her room. She worked at the hotel after all. But she certainly wasn't on the housekeeping staff so why had she needed to come in here?

Jenna refused to let this question dampen her buoyant mood. She had a house to furnish and a credit card with a satisfyingly large credit limit. Opening her laptop she started working down her list of household essentials.

It felt like only minutes later when there was a tap on her door so Jenna was amazed when she glanced at the clock on the laptop screen and noticed two hours had passed.

Blinking as her eyes adjusted to the dim light in the room she hurried to the door, remembering at the last second to check through the spy hole to see who was there. Her tummy did that flip that was becoming familiar when she saw it was Alex.

'Hey, Jenna,' he said with a beaming smile. 'I wondered if you had plans for dinner tonight. If not, the chef's doing a beach barbecue if you'd like to come with me.'

Jenna was confused. Was this the same Alex who'd warned her off when she tried to kiss him the other evening? They'd agreed to be just friends but now he was asking her to join him for dinner. Christina wouldn't be happy.

Although Jenna had promised herself she wouldn't allow Christina to warn her off, it didn't make sense to deliberately antagonise her. Alex's next words made his invitation a little less mysterious.

'Christina's out with her father,' he said. 'They have a monthly meeting to make sure the hotel's doing OK. She's the manager but he's still very much in charge.'

Jenna thought the suggestion over quickly. What harm could it do if she and Alex went to the barbecue? No doubt they'd be surrounded by a crowd of people so it wasn't as if anything untoward could happen.

As soon as she'd thought it Jenna realised that 'something untoward' was exactly what she wished could happen. She closed down that line of thinking immediately.

'I'd love to come,' she said. 'Give me half an hour and I'll be ready.'

'Half an hour?' Alex said with a laugh. 'Christina needs at least two hours' notice before she'll go any-where.'

Jenna smiled but as she closed the door on Alex she thought about those words. They summed up the difference between the two women. Jenna, the low-maintenance girl and Christina, the glamorous, beautiful woman. She sighed as she headed for the shower.

★   ★   ★

Christina and her father were seated at their usual table in one of the most exclusive restaurants in Tampa. His driver had picked Christina up and they'd called for Mr Mitchell at his luxury apartment on the way to the restaurant.

As always, they'd said little to each other on the journey, besides asking after each other's health. Business conversation could wait until they'd chosen their meals from the menu and Mr Mitchell had chosen a fine wine to accompany their food. At last it was time for their odd version of a board meeting to start.

'So, princess, how's business?' Mr Mitchell said.

'Absolutely fine, Daddy, like I tell you every month. You can see the figures for yourself and it seems like you drop into the hotel whenever you like. I don't know why you insist on these meetings.'

'When would I see you if I didn't insist? You always seem to be too busy when I drop in, as you call it,' he said.

The slight smile on his face told Christina he was teasing. He knew she would make time to see him even if they didn't have the regular dinner meetings. And she knew he just enjoyed giving her a lavish dinner once a month that was tax deductible.

Halfway down her first glass of wine Christina started to relax. The crisp, smooth taste of the exquisite Chablis was just what she needed after the past few days. She would let her father enjoy a couple of glasses before she brought up the subject that was bothering her.

Her father's choice of wine that night gave a clue to his personality. Woe betide the wine waiter who questioned Bernie Mitchell's choice of white wine when they were both going to eat red meat. As he was cutting into his blue fillet steak Christina judged the time was right.

'Daddy, there's something I need to talk to you about. It's not the business, it's something else.' He looked up at her warily but as he was chewing his steak he didn't answer and Christina went on.

'It's Alex. This woman from his past has turned up and I'm worried he's going to dump me.'

Her father washed down the mouthful of steak and looked Christina straight in the eye, pointing at her with his knife.

'He wouldn't dare,' he said at last. 'I'd have him out of a job so fast his head would spin.'

'I know, Daddy, and thank you for that,' Christina said in her best princess daughter voice. 'But it's not really him, it's her. She's going to try and take him away from me, I just know it.'

A single tear ran down her cheek and she let it fall and drip on to the table. She'd perfected this crying trick years ago and it never failed to get through to her father.

'Oh, darling, don't cry,' he said, in a voice his business associates wouldn't recognise. Everyone knew Christina was Mitchell's Achilles heel. 'Tell me what you want me to do, and consider it done.'

Christina let a silence hang in the air to make it seem as if she was thinking about his offer. It wouldn't go down well with him if it looked as though she'd already expected his help. Better to let him think she'd felt helpless before his intervention.

If there was one thing her father enjoyed more that seeing her happy it was knowing that he himself had been the cause of that happiness. It had been the pattern of her childhood after her parents had split up.

Christina's mother had given up trying to compete with the gifts Bernie would buy for Christmas and birthdays. But what Christina was about to ask for was a world away from the lavish toys and gadgets of her youth.

'Well . . . ' she said eventually. 'If there was anything you could do to make this woman move on it would certainly be a big help. She's been talking about finding a house near the hotel and I don't think I could cope with knowing she was nearby.'

Mitchell thought for a few minutes then smiled and nodded.

'I'm sure I can sort something out. It wouldn't be the first time I've, er, encouraged someone to leave town when they'd been planning to stay.'

Christina didn't want to think about that too much. It was all very well having a job and home provided by her father but she never wanted to know the details of how he'd become so successful.

She'd always thought he was happy working for the hotel chain back in the day but then suddenly everything had changed. He'd made some very influential contacts during his years as a troubleshooter in the hotel business.

Christina didn't know exactly how he'd got into a position where he could start buying hotels rather than just sorting out their problems.

She knew there was something shady about it but her father had never confided in her. Whenever she had tried to become involved in that side of the business Bernie had always warned her off and eventually she'd given up.

'So should I just leave it with you, then?' she asked now. She was disappointed that she wouldn't be getting her own hands dirty, so to speak, but mostly she was relieved that getting rid of Jenna was something she could stand back and watch.

'You'll need a few details, I suppose.

Her name is Jenna Logan and she's currently staying in one of the guest huts at the hotel.'

Christina stopped speaking as she noticed the expression on her father's face change. Instead of the determined look in his eyes of a few moments earlier he looked stunned. The colour drained from his face and he grabbed for his wine glass, annoyed to find it empty.

'Waiter — double scotch. Now!' he shouted.

Christina was amazed. She'd never seen him react like that in her life.

'What's up, Daddy?' she asked.

'Nothing, nothing,' he said, wiping the sweat from his brow with his napkin.

'Logan, you say? What else do you know about her? Where's she from?'

'New York,' Christina said. 'She turned up here a few days ago hoping for a joyous reunion with Alex. She and her family used to holiday at the hotel years ago. Why? What's the problem?'

'I said it's nothing,' Mitchell said, at last starting to recover something of his composure. 'But listen, I might have been a bit hasty when I said I could help you get rid of this Jenna Logan.'

Christina couldn't believe what she was hearing. Never in her life had her father failed to provide exactly what she demanded. And because it had never happened before she had no idea what to do.

She stood abruptly, sending her chair screeching backwards across the wood floor. Flinging her napkin on to her still half full plate, Christina fled from the restaurant, only realising when she was outside that her father's car wasn't due to pick them up for another hour.

Christina was boiling with rage. How dare her father offer to deal with the situation only to whisk the offer away minutes later? She was now even more determined to make Jenna Logan suffer, no matter what it took. As she stalked back inside to ask someone to call her a taxi another thought struck her. The name Logan had been what had affected her father badly. And Christina was going to find out why.

The Awful Truth

This was a night of firsts for Bernie Mitchell. It was the first time he'd tried this restaurant. It was the first time his daughter had ever walked out on him. And it was the first time he'd thought about the Logan family for many years.

It was a measure of his unease that he hadn't immediately followed his daughter and pulled her up for her disrespectful behaviour. After all he'd done for her over the years, how dare she walk away from him and leave him as the object of his fellow diners' curiosity?

After the divorce they'd become a team. Bernie and Christina Mitchell against the world. But all along the unspoken rule was that Daddy knew best.

Once she'd graduated from high school Christina had gone to the business school Bernie had picked out for her. Only after finishing top of her class there had he taken her into the business and set her up as the manager of his flagship hotel.

It had been a great decision. Christina ensured the place ran like clockwork and the hotel was running at almost full capacity all the time. She had come up with some great ideas for expansion that had made the hotel even more profitable.

Bernie must have been more shaken by the Logan name than he'd realised because, unusually for him, he started to question whether he'd praised his daughter enough for her good work. He'd never seen her in such an emotional state as she'd been tonight. Was the hotel too much for her?

No, Bernie decided. Christina's mood was nothing to do with her job. It was that Alex Shepherd who was to blame. When Christina had told him she was seeing Alex he'd been disappointed at first.

Then after a while it seemed Alex made Christina happy so he left them to it. Now it looked as though his initial reaction had been the right one.

Shepherd came from a family of under achievers and he was totally unsuited to Bernie's high-flying daughter. Well, maybe this Jenna Logan had come along at the right time. If she broke the couple up and Christina went on to find someone better Bernie, for one, would be happy.

But why did it have to be a Logan that was involved? Bernie tried to calm himself down. He pushed away his plate, having finished his steak. Nothing, but nothing, ever put him off his food.

Now he was thinking more calmly he realised Logan was a pretty common name. Maybe this Jenna was nothing to do with the Logans he'd . . . he'd what? Dealt with, was the only way he could put it.

But hadn't Christina said Jenna Logan used to come to the St Pete hotel with her parents? What were the chances it was a coincidence?

Bernie signalled the waiter and asked for his dessert to be brought immediately. He had work to do, and fast. But not so fast that he couldn't enjoy his chocolate pudding.

★   ★   ★

An hour later, Bernie Mitchell was sitting at his desk in the study of his apartment. He worked at home most of the time these days, not seeing the point of commuting to a corporate office, wasting half his day in traffic.

Most of his work could be done using modern technology and he even conducted most face to face meetings via the internet. Only when a client or supplier preferred wining and dining did he leave his large penthouse.

It had only taken him minutes to confirm that Jenna Logan was the daughter of Paul and Karen Logan from New York. He sat pondering the implications for a few moments then searched his phone contacts.

If he pressed the call button he might be signing Jenna Logan's death warrant. His thumb hovered over the button as he drifted back in time.

Bernie would probably have carried on in his career as a hotel troubleshooter indefinitely if it hadn't been for the divorce. His ex-wife's lawyer had wiped the floor with Bernie's own legal advisor, though, and by the time the dust had settled he was trying to support Christina on a fraction of his previous earnings.

After a few months, he realised things would have to change. He'd been offered work by several of his influential contacts over the years and it was time to think about a career change.

Looking back now, Bernie couldn't believe how naive he'd been. He'd taken up an offer that allowed him to stay connected to what he knew — the hotel business — while bringing in an income that allowed him and Christina to live in style.

It all seemed so simple at first. He was the front man who would negotiate buying a hotel on behalf of his employer. Then, without too much work on his side, he'd move on to the next deal, and the next. It took him about a year to realise he was actually the front man for a money laundering scheme.

His bosses were making their money from drugs, prostitution and illegal gambling, then 'cleaning' their dirty money buying legitimate businesses which they'd then sell on, even if it was at a loss.

Bernie took some sick days when he learned the truth. He had to think about what he should do. In the end, though, the decision was quite simple. He couldn't get out of his current job without his bosses questioning his loyalty. And Bernie had heard what happened to disloyal people in this business.

He stayed with the organisation, telling himself he had no choice. He was doing it for Christina because she would be in danger if he tried to leave. In that way he quietened his conscience but he had no idea just what demands would be put on him the longer he stayed.

Things came to a head a couple of years later. Bernie was summoned to an office in Miami with no clue as to what the meeting was about. It felt like something out of *The Godfather* when he was ushered into a wood-lined board room and invited to sit at one end of a polished table. The figure at the other end of the table sized him up for a minute before speaking.

'I have a job for you,' the person said. No introductions, no preamble. 'And a proposition. You do this job and we'll cut you free with enough capital to start up on your own.'

Bernie gulped. He had to say something or he'd look stupid.

'And if I don't do the job?'

The other person smiled, though it seemed their face wasn't used to expressing pleasure.

'If you don't do the job you can say goodbye to your daughter.'

Bernie's heart was racing as he listened to the details of what he was expected to do. Apparently he was the ideal person because he'd never been in trouble with the law, unlike the majority of the other employees of the organisation. He knew he had no choice. They'd found his weak spot.

Faced with the thought of putting Christina in danger he developed tunnel vision. He didn't even consider the idea of going to the police. Thinking back now, he still stood by his actions in that regard. He'd learned since that half the police department were in the pocket of his boss at that time.

Bernie was responsible for arranging the job he'd been given and he knew he'd planned and carried it out to perfection. Nobody had ever suspected that the car crash that killed Paul and Karen Logan was anything but a tragic accident.

With his payout Bernie had bought the hotel on St Pete Beach. The timing had been perfect. The Shepherds were so desperate for money to pay medical expenses they sold up for half what the place was worth.

Bernie had no qualms about it. He didn't have a conscience any more. OK, he'd let Alex Shepherd stay on at the hotel out of a touch of sentiment but having said that, the lad was a good worker. If only he hadn't set his sights on Christina.

Bernie ran his hands through his hair. This evening had gone full circle. First Christina had complained to him about Jenna Logan trying to take Alex from her, and now he was sitting here wishing Alex wasn't with Christina at all.

He had to admit it was a little confusing. His head was telling him to get rid of Jenna Logan for good. His heart was suggesting it might be a better idea to let her stay around and break up Alex and Christina.

As usual, Bernie's head won the argument. He was owed a few favours by some very influential people. It was time to call those favours in and get some help with how to dispose of Jenna Logan before she got curious about what had happened to her parents.

Sinister Plans

Jenna's rental car had been dropped off and she decided to spend the day revisiting some of the places she and her parents had enjoyed in the past. She'd sat with a map over breakfast plotting a route.

The more she thought about it, the more Jenna was convinced that she would be staying around here for a long time.

Maybe she'd try to track down some of the people her parents had known in the old days and perhaps even work out what had led to their final trip.

Although as she thought about trying to find people, she realised her parents hadn't really ever spoken about any friends here.

While she had been bonding with Alex and his family, her parents had always travelled around as a couple, never really socialising considering they were supposed to be on holiday.

Just as she was about to set off she heard a shout behind her.

'Jenna, wait up.' It was Alex, running up from the direction of his dive school hut. 'I just had my only group today cancel on me,' he said. 'Food poisoning, apparently. Not from here,' he added quickly. 'Anyway, it means I'm at a loose end. Fancy some company?'

'I'm not sure Christina would be impressed,' Jenna said, noticing a dark shadow flit over Alex's face at her words.

'It's fine,' he said. 'I'm not supposed to be working in the hotel today, anyway. She won't miss me.'

Jenna knew he was deliberately ignoring what she meant but it wasn't up to her to spell it out. It was so confusing how one minute Alex was keen to spend time with her and the next he was backing off.

Once again, Jenna had the little debate in her head about whether it was all right to spend time with Alex even though his girlfriend had told her not to. As usual the rebel within her won the argument.

'OK, a little local knowledge wouldn't do any harm,' she said. 'I'd already planned a route but you can be my tour guide instead.'

It really hadn't been too hard a decision to make and now Jenna was elated at the prospect of spending a few hours with Alex.

They set off without a backward glance at the hotel. Christina was watching them go with an expression on her face that would have done a Disney villain proud.

She slammed the office door behind her when she went back inside. Somebody was going to feel the heat of her temper.

There was something she had to do first, though. She should have done it the previous night really, she knew.

She took a few moments to calm down and regulate her breathing, then picked up her phone and tapped to make a video call to her father.

'Daddy, I'm sorry,' she said as soon as he answered. She was relieved to see she hadn't disturbed his breakfast.

Christina could see the small image of herself in the corner of the phone screen and made sure she had the right kind of contrite expression.

'It was wrong of me to cause a scene in the restaurant and talk to you like that.'

Bernie smiled as he listened. He'd picked up his phone to call her a dozen times but stopped himself. It had to be Christina who made the first move. In their power-play relationship it had always been the same.

Christina wasn't sure whether to admit to what she had set in motion earlier that morning but she couldn't resist the temptation to tell her father she was trying to sort something out for herself at last.

'That's my girl,' Bernie said when she'd confided in him. His own plans for Jenna Logan could be kept in reserve. He had faith in his daughter — he had taught her everything she needed to know, after all — but it never did any harm to have a backup plan.

Raised Eyebrows

The nearby town was the only densely populated area on the strip of land that ran parallel to a large section of the west coast of the state of Florida.

There were a couple of shopping malls and several hotels and high-rise apartment blocks as well as an upmarket housing development next to a golf course. The most used connection to the mainland was the bridge Jenna had travelled over by bus a few days earlier.

Most of the countryside was fairly flat, with just one hilly area to the north, and Jenna and Alex decided to start their road trip to the south of the town then head north before returning to the hotel.

'I never really had chance to explore when I was younger,' Jenna said. 'Do you remember how I used to spend all my time following you around until you'd finished all your chores and we could spend the rest of the day together?'

'Of course I remember,' Alex said. Jenna could feel him staring at her and she was glad she had the excuse of needing to keep her eyes on the road. She knew her face would give away her feelings, which were showing themselves more and more the longer she was in Alex's company.

'You know, I was thinking earlier, when I look back I can't remember spending that much time with my parents on those holidays,' Jenna said.

'Yet over the years since they died it's as if I've filled in the gaps by pretending I was with them most of the time. I realise now, though, that the photo I always keep by my bed is the only one with all three of us together. How weird is that?'

'Not weird, really,' Alex said. 'And if you really only have one family holiday photo I reckon I was the photographer.'

'Really?'

'Yeah. I remember it well. It was the first time you came here. Your dad handed me his camera and asked me to take a picture. That's how we got talking and in no time we were getting on like a house on fire. I'm glad you still have the photo.'

Jenna smiled. She remembered now too. She'd liked Alex immediately. She vaguely remembered hearing her mother say how cute she and Alex looked as they wandered towards the beach together.

She felt a warm glow inside at the memory of her mother's voice, especially as it was connected to herself and Alex.

After driving around for several miles, stopping occasionally to admire the beautiful scenery, Alex suggested they should stop for coffee at a place owned by a friend of his.

Alex was obviously well known there, judging by all the greetings he received and Jenna noticed raised eyebrows amongst the customers and staff.

It didn't take her long to work out that the reactions were due to Alex being with her instead of Christina. Alex and Christina had been dating for quite a while now and it was bound to seem odd to their friends that Alex was here with a strange woman.

'I hope this isn't going to cause you a problem,' she said in a whisper as they sat down. Quickly following that thought, she silently hoped it wasn't going to cause herself a problem, either. Christina had been pretty clear in her warnings.

Alex brushed her concern aside but she could tell he hadn't anticipated what people might think. From the corner of her eye Jenna saw one of the waitresses tapping a message into her phone. Could she be alerting Christina? Jenna wasn't usually so paranoid but this situation was definitely starting to make her feel that way.

'Maybe we should make it a quick coffee,' she said. 'I have a to-do list a mile long and I still want to explore up north before we go back.'

Alex's phone beeped and he glanced at the screen before turning it over on the table. Their drinks arrived and Alex's phone continued to beep as they hastily drank their delicious coffee.

Despite their easy conversation all the way here in the car they now sat in silence. When Alex made a quick trip to the bathroom Jenna couldn't resist the temptation and she quickly picked up his phone.

Six messages, all from Christina. The one showing on the screen simply said, 'Get back here now.'

★ ★ ★

Christina stared at her phone screen for a full five minutes before she realised Alex wasn't going to reply to any of her messages. This was a first. Throughout their relationship she'd been able to rely on one thing. If she said jump, Alex would ask how high.

Now, within days of Jenna Logan

appearing he'd started to ignore her. She'd sent those messages trying to get Alex to come back to the hotel for a reason. As a warning. But she couldn't spell out exactly why the warning was needed without incriminating herself. What a mess.

Christina scrolled through her phone contacts until she found the person she suddenly desperately needed to speak to. When he picked up she spoke before he even had a chance to say hello.

'Did you do as I asked?' she said quickly.

'Of course I did. Why wouldn't I?'

Christina didn't bother to answer, ending the call abruptly. What was she supposed to do now?

Terror Behind the Wheel

Alex had taken over the driving after they left the coffee shop. It gave Jenna a chance to relax, look around and enjoy the scenery and they both felt a little foolish for not suggesting these driving arrangements from the start.

The rental car was nothing special but Alex didn't get the chance to drive very often these days and he enjoyed taking the wheel.

Every so often he took a diversion along roads that were barely more than dirt tracks which Jenna would never have known existed but they led to some of the most breathtaking scenery in the area.

'I used to come up here with my friends all the time,' he said and Jenna interpreted the wistful look on his face as meaning he wasn't allowed to spend much time with his friends any more.

Was that because he was always working or because Christina had banned him from seeing them, too?

They were almost at the furthest north point and they'd been steadily climbing for a few miles. Alex knew the area like the back of his hand and as he turned the final bend he parked just off the roadway.

'Come on,' he said. 'I wouldn't forgive myself if we came all the way up here and I didn't show you this.'

They climbed out of the car and walked to the edge beyond the other side of the road. Jenna gasped as she looked out at the view.

'It's beautiful,' was all she could come up with, but it didn't do justice to the glorious stretch of land and sea beneath them.

They stood looking out to sea for a few moments and when Jenna looked down and saw her hand in Alex's she wasn't sure who had made the first move to hold hands. She didn't care. It felt good and it felt right.

For the past few days her feelings toward Alex had been in confusion but now she was sure. She wouldn't do anything about it because he was with Christina. It wasn't so much that Christina had warned her off in no uncertain terms, it was more that Jenna herself knew her own boundaries of right and wrong and it was time to stick to them.

She gently pulled her hand away and returned to the car. Alex followed her as if he was snapping out of thoughts that had transported him.

Soon they were setting off back down the winding road.

They'd been chatting continually all the time they'd been together, until that shared moment looking at the breathtaking view, but now suddenly Alex had fallen silent.

Jenna glanced at him and saw by the frown on his face there was something wrong. As always, she instantly assumed that whatever was bothering another person was her fault.

'What is it, Alex?' she asked. 'Have I said something to upset you?'

No response. It was only then Jenna realised the car had noticeably picked up speed, even though they were negotiating some tight bends on the steep road.

'Alex, what's wrong with the car?' she asked, her voice higher pitched now.

'I don't know,' he said at last. 'The brakes aren't responding. I'm trying to keep control but I'm scared the car's running away with me.'

Alex's panicked words about the brakes were the last thing he said for what seemed like ages to Jenna. His concentration was now focused completely on driving safely and somehow getting them both out of the car alive.

It was pure luck that Alex had taken over the driving as he knew the roads so well. If Jenna had still been behind the wheel they would have crashed by now for sure.

She thought fleetingly of her parents, wondering if this was the same stretch of treacherous road where their lives had ended. She'd never wanted to know the precise location of their accident — never been one of those people who were compelled to bring floral tributes to an accident site. Now, though, she feared she might share her parents' fate.

Somehow Alex managed to negotiate several bends, where he purposely steered the car right next to the metal crash barrier at the edge of the road.

One slight miscalculation and the car could have ploughed through the barrier, its momentum only slowed a little by the metal.

Instead, Alex skilfully touched the barrier side-on so that, with a horrific screech of metal on metal and a shower of sparks, the vehicle's speed slowed slightly with each touch.

As the gradient of the hill levelled gradually, Alex managed to steer towards a lay-by where there were bushes and undergrowth to one side. The car finally came to a stop facing into the bushes.

Jenna was shaking as she looked at Alex, his head down on his hands on the steering wheel. They sat silently for a few moments then it was Alex who spoke first.

'You'd better call the car rental people,' he said, a slight breathlessness the only thing giving away the ordeal they'd just survived.

Shock Realisation

It was an hour before the car rental company's recovery truck arrived. They'd offered to bring a replacement car but Jenna knew she wouldn't feel like driving again that day and she didn't want to put Alex in a position where he had to, either. She decided she could do without a car until she could find one to buy.

For some reason their close call had planted it firmly in her mind that she was staying round here for good. While they'd been waiting she and Alex had discussed what had happened.

'Virtually new cars don't have their brakes fail like that,' Alex said.

'What are you saying?' Jenna said. 'You think someone tampered with the brakes deliberately?'

'It's possible,' Alex said.

'But I'd been driving it for hours and it was fine.'

'If someone cut the brake line the brakes wouldn't fail immediately,' Alex said. 'It would take a while for the fluid to drain and you wouldn't realise there was a problem until you needed to slam on your brakes. It's our bad luck that didn't happen until we were coming down this steep road.'

'But why would anyone do that to my car?' Jenna said. Alex didn't answer. He didn't want to face the possibility that had started to take shape in his head.

When the recovery vehicle driver dropped them both off at the hotel Alex went straight to the office. Jenna assumed he was needed at work, though the way he left her so abruptly struck her as strange after the experience they'd been through.

Jenna went to her guest hut and stood for a few minutes under the power shower. The massaging effect of the needles of hot water relaxed her tense shoulders and helped to counter-act the effects of the adrenaline overload she'd just suffered.

After her shower Jenna started to think clearly and logically. The most likely reason for what she and Alex had just been through was simply a mechanical or parts failure of the car even though it was almost brand new. She called the rental company.

'Hi, it's Jenna Logan.' She listened for a moment as the person on the other end of the call apologised profusely for what had happened. They were probably afraid she was going to sue the company or something, Jenna realised.

'Look,' she said eventually, worried they would never shut up. 'I just want to know what was wrong with the car. As soon as you find out please let me know.'

Having been assured they would be in touch, Jenna felt calmer. Her thought was that she would be able to put Alex's mind at rest about it being targeted at her. She hadn't been around long enough to make any enemies so how could it have been?

An image of Christina's frowning face flitted through Jenna's mind but she shook her head.

OK, the other woman had warned her off Alex a couple of times but surely she couldn't hate Jenna enough to endanger her life, could she?

Before she put her mind to anything else, like more shopping for her new house, Jenna decided to send an e-mail to the manager of the car rental company confirming what they'd just discussed.

She always liked to be able to back up anything important in writing and she knew it would be at the back of her mind all the time until she did it.

Five minutes later she'd typed a couple of lines documenting what had happened with the car, and sent the message.

It was only after she'd signed off and closed her laptop that she realised she hadn't looked at her *Like!* magazine work for a while.

She grabbed the small computer and headed to the beach bar.

A few minutes later, a cup of their delicious aromatic coffee in front of her, Jenna signed in to her work e-mails. What she saw left her stunned.

A message that had been created just minutes earlier was at the top of the list. At first Jenna couldn't understand how it had appeared directly rather than being forwarded by the editor.

Usually her editor forwarded messages to her so there could be a delay of hours or even days before Jenna saw them.

Then she realised what had happened. Her editor had taken the week off and when she did that, messages were automatically sent straight to Jenna.

Anyway, it wasn't so much how recently the message had been sent as its content that worried her: 'Dear Jenna, I've just had a near-death experience and I don't know who to talk to about it. My car went out of control on a hill and nearly crashed. How will I get over the shock? Love, Nonnie x.'

Jenna's mind was racing. She'd decided to put the previous odd messages down to coincidence but this was too much. And that weird name — Nonnie — hadn't that been the name on the first message, the one about the failed proposal?

An unwanted solution started to force itself into Jenna's consciousness. She'd had enough of this and she had plenty going on in her life at the moment. Was it time to end Ask Jenna?

Only the thought of all the young people she'd helped through the column in the past stopped her firing off a resignation e-mail immediately.

She'd think it through calmly for a while before she did anything. And anyway, as her editor wasn't around for a few days she wouldn't get the e-mail yet.

Jenna was finally starting to learn that impulsive decisions didn't always turn out for the best. Understatement of the century, she thought.

Then another, frightening, thought occurred to her. Was she growing up at last? Jenna laughed at herself. At least she could still put a humorous spin on things.

★　★　★

Alex slammed the office door behind him, his face like thunder. Christina stood up from her chair, determined to take the initiative in this confrontation.

'Why didn't you reply to my messages?' she said.

The look of confusion on Alex's face told her she'd been right to get in first. But Alex wasn't about to be put off from what he'd come here to say.

Christina had never seen him like this before. Despite the seriousness of the situation she felt a thrill of attraction course through her body.

'Never mind your messages,' Alex said. 'I'm going to ask you something and I want the truth. Do you understand?'

'Yes, of course,' Christina said. It didn't come naturally to her to allow someone else to dominate a conversation but she forced herself to bite her tongue. 'Sit down, Alex,' she simply added, 'you should take it easy after what's happened.'

Alex continued to stand, clenching and unclenching his hands.

'Did you arrange for someone to damage Jenna's rental car?'

'What?' Christina said. 'How could you suggest such a thing?'

Alex looked at her for several seconds. He knew his girlfriend could be untruthful and sly at times but he'd never known her lie to his face. Without definite evidence that she'd been involved he'd have to believe her.

He turned on his heel and left the office. It was only later, when he was working in the dive school hut that it struck him.

'Take it easy after what's happened,' Christina had said. How had she known?

Words of Love

At last Jenna had the keys to her new home and since she didn't really have much to move apart from the couple of bags she'd arrived here with, she decided she might as well check out of the hotel and move in to the house immediately.

The other thing she'd managed to get hold of was her new phone. She headed out to the beach in search of Alex at the dive school, thinking that even if he wasn't there she could put the dive school number into her phone.

Her luck was in, though. He was there doing some maintenance jobs.

'Hey,' Jenna said as she drew nearer.

'Hey, yourself,' Alex said, a beaming grin on his face.

Jenna wondered if he bestowed that grin on everyone or saved it for her but then she told herself off for being silly.

Every time she saw Alex it was as if she was propelled back in time to when she was a teenager.

Now even her thoughts were being translated to teen-think. They were both adults now and she should remember that. Oh yes, and Alex had a girlfriend, as if Jenna could ever be allowed to forget.

'I'll be leaving soon,' Jenna said. 'And I just wanted to put your number in my phone, if that's OK.'

'Of course it's OK. Here.' Alex reached for the phone and tapped his number in. Jenna found herself glancing over her shoulder in case Christina was watching them. Then she scolded herself. She refused to be told who she could and could not be friends with by that woman.

'Do you need any help moving?' Alex asked.

'It's not as if I have much to take with me.' Jenna laughed. But then a thought struck her. 'If you have a little time, though, I'd appreciate some

107

company while I get some supplies in. Most of the furniture is being delivered over the next few days but I've still got to eat in the meantime.'

'Sure, let me finish up here and I'll be with you. But . . . ' He stopped.

'But don't let Christina know?' Jenna said and Alex bowed his head.

'It's just not worth the hassle of her finding out,' he said. 'I'm not going to let her stop me being friends with you but there's no point telling her I'm coming with you now.'

It echoed what Jenna had been thinking just moments earlier. At least they were both on the same page.

An hour later Jenna handed in her key at reception, saying a silent prayer of thanks that Christina wasn't manning the front desk at the time. She could do without seeing her just now.

Then, after a quick trip into town for food shopping, when Jenna had spent half the time looking around to see if any of Alex's friends had spotted them, she let them both into the beach house where she was looking forward to spending the next few months.

After stashing away the supplies in cupboards she reached out two cold bottles of beer from a cool bag and opened the French doors that led out to her section of the beach.

'It's paradise,' she said a few minutes later. The sun was warming her body and the cold beer was a refreshing contrast

'Yep. It's what I've been telling people all my life,' Alex said. 'I don't know why anyone wants to live anywhere else.'

'But you've never actually been anywhere else,' Jenna pointed out.

'I have,' Alex said, an indignant tone in his voice.

'School field trips don't count.' Jenn laughed. She was relieved when Alex laughed too as she'd suddenly worried he might think she was belittling his parochial attitude to life. After all, maybe he was right. If you live in paradise why would you ever want to go anywhere else?

Jenna had always loved her New York home but the months she'd spent in Florida growing up were actually the happiest times of her life.

Alex's phone beeped with a text and he reluctantly drew it out of his shorts pocket, shaking his head as he read the message.

'Christina?' Jenna asked and he nodded.

'Just the usual. Where am I? When will I be back? And so on and so on.'

The words 'trouble in paradise' jumped into Jenna's head but she just managed to stop herself saying them. It wasn't up to her to point out what she saw as Christina's controlling attitude to Alex. He'd either work it out for himself or live this way for ever.

Up to him, she thought, but she couldn't stop other thoughts crowding in. Like what if there was no Christina? What if Jenna and Alex could pick up where they left off years ago? She shook her head as if she could physically shake off the thoughts.

It took her a few minutes to realise that Alex hadn't immediately jumped up to comply with Christina's orders in her text. If anything, he seemed to have settled in more determinedly. Well, she thought, I might as well take advantage of the opportunity for company.

'Would you like to stay for dinner?' she asked, watching Alex's reaction closely. Of course, even if he decided to stay it might just be because he'd seen the amazing steaks she'd just bought.

'I would. I would like that very much,' he said and Jenna felt the usual butterflies in the tummy thing. But seconds later Alex made her face up to reality. 'But, Jenna, we can't always have what we want, can we?'

Alex finished his beer and got up to walk round the front of the house. Jenna followed and suddenly Alex turned back to her and she walked right into him. They both laughed as he put his hands around her waist and they smiled into each other's eyes. A kiss was surely inevitable, Jenna thought and raised her face up to his. Alex gave her a quick kiss on the cheek followed by a tight hug.

'I love you, Jenna,' he said, the words muffled because his lips were pressed against her hair. 'You're my first love and I'll always feel this way about you. But . . . '

'But Christina,' Jenna finished for him. She just wanted Alex to go now so she could work out how she was feeling. He said he loved her and he always would. She knew she loved him, too. It should all be so simple. Instead, she was feeling more confused than ever.

All Too Much

Jenna watched Alex drive away then went inside in search of her laptop. The best way she knew to sort through something like this was to write up her journal. Seeing the words appear on the screen somehow made them more real.

Half an hour later she closed the computer and sighed. It hadn't worked as well as usual but at least she felt as if she understood her own side of things better, even if she still had no idea where she stood with Alex.

Christina was his girlfriend but that didn't mean he was committed to her for life. It would be different if they were married or even engaged. Jenna would never dream of starting a relationship with a man under those circumstances. But as things stood she and Alex had no commitments or responsibilities.

If he wanted to, he could end things with Christina and be with Jenna. Perhaps it was all too soon. It was less than a week since she'd burst back into his life, after all.

The more she thought about it, the more Jenna realised she should take a step backwards and concentrate on what she had rented this house for in the first place.

Her priority should be to work on her writing and developing her career. Like she was always telling her teenage followers on the magazine, life was about more than romance.

Jenna laughed to herself as she pondered the need to take a bit of her own medicine. For the last couple of years she'd been in a relationship with Shaun that she now saw had never been going anywhere.

All that time she'd been dishing out advice to young women and girls who looked to her as a role model. Not for the first time she questioned her credentials for the Ask Jenna job.

For her own peace of mind, Jenna resolved to stick to what she had just decided. She would work hard and keep out of Alex's way as much as possible. There should be no need to cross paths with him unless she wanted to. Her lack of willpower showed when she immediately admitted to herself that was exactly what she did want.

It was so annoying that no matter how much her sensible side told her to stay away from Alex, with all her heart she wanted to follow him right now. Was he with Christina by now? Jenna thought she would explode with jealousy at the thought. Great start to the new resolution.

Before switching her laptop off, Jenna decided to take a quick look at her e-mails. She wasn't in the mood for answering any Ask Jenna questions but she liked to keep on top of the number of e-mails that were piling up.

One of the new messages leaped out from the screen at her. It wasn't the anonymous Nonnie this time but the sender's name certainly piqued her interest. It was from Shaun.

'Jenna — I've been trying to call you for days, why won't you answer? You know how much I hate e-mail.'

Jenna knew Shaun disliked e-mail and texting because your words could so easily be misunderstood. He liked face-to-face talking, or phone calls at least. But of course she had made that impossible by ditching her mobile phone the night she left New York. He hadn't been on her priority list for sharing her new number.

The e-mail continued: 'Anyway, please can you reply so I at least know you're safe? Erica says she hasn't heard from you, either, and you'd been so close lately we're really worried.'

Jenna felt a pang of guilt as she realised she should have got in touch but she'd felt so humiliated after that night she'd just wanted to put everything behind her, including her closest friends. She made a mental note to get in touch with her uncle tomorrow, too.

He might be as worried as Shaun.

For now she typed a hasty reply, telling Shaun she was OK. Within two minutes a reply came back and it was clear Shaun wasn't looking for any reconciliation.

'Jenna. Thanks for letting us know you're alive, at least. I think it's best if we end things now. I don't see a way back from this. It's been coming for a while. Shaun.'

Jenna was stunned. She knew she'd been selfish running away from the situation she'd created at the basketball game but what did he mean it had been coming for a while?

She'd had no clue Shaun was thinking about ending their relationship. Would she have even contemplated proposing if she'd had an inkling?

She thought back over the past few months. Things had been plodding along as usual. Maybe that was the problem — she wasn't exciting enough. But Erica had constantly told Jenna she thought she was the ideal woman for her brother. Once she'd got over her initial dislike for Jenna, that is.

Had Jenna allowed Erica's assurances to make her blind to the fact Shaun wanted out of the relationship?

Well, at least they agreed on one thing — there really was no way back from her failed proposal and the way she had reacted by running away.

Maybe she should have stayed in New York and faced up to things. The mature thing to do would have been to talk to Shaun and end the relationship amicably. But since when had she ever done the mature thing?

If she'd felt confused earlier with Alex, now she was totally baffled. Once again the thoughts of whether she should give up the Ask Jenna work bounced round her head. And that reminded her to check her work messages. As she'd feared there was now a message from Nonnie.

'Dear Jenna, I'm so confused. My ex has told me he wanted to finish with me months ago and the other man in my life has gone back to his girlfriend . . . '

Jenna didn't even finish reading the message. She felt like throwing her laptop across the room and smashing it. This was too much. It was as if this Nonnie was inside her head, echoing everything that was happening to her. But Jenna had no idea what to do about it. Her editor was still on holiday so there was no way to stop the messages coming straight through to Jenna's account.

In the end the answer was obvious. It was time to take a few sick days. She was certainly owed some.

Jenna typed a quick message to her editor, pleading the flu, and an automated response to all e-mails stating Ask Jenna was closed for a week. Jenna felt relieved once she'd done that.

She could concentrate all her effort on an idea she had come up with earlier. She was going to convert her journal into a blog — with the highly unoriginal name 'Ask Jenna'.

She'd had the idea floating around in

the back of her mind for a while after rumours that *Like!* magazine was struggling for reader numbers. If it went under, Jenna thought she might be able to combine the advice column with the blog. But starting the project could wait until tomorrow. It was time to try and enjoy her first night in her new home.

Dramatic Change of Plan

Alex drove back to the hotel on autopilot. His mind was going over and over the situation he'd found himself in over the last few days. How could someone he hadn't seen for over ten years turn up and turn his whole life upside down?

He'd thought about Jenna Logan a lot over the years, of course he had. She was his first love, after all. But as time went by it was only when a particular song that had been a hit during one of their summers together came on the radio, or he caught a scent similar to the apple shampoo she always used — things like that would jog his memory.

Otherwise he could go for weeks or even months at a time without thinking about Jenna and wondering where she was, what she was doing, who she was with.

The only person he'd ever been able to talk about it to was his kid sister, Amber. His brothers would have made his life hell if they'd known he was still pining for a girl he would probably never see again. But Amber would listen to him without trying to offer any advice or making fun of him.

He remembered their last conversation on the subject. It was just before Alex started seeing Christina.

'I'm thinking of asking Christina Mitchell on a date. What do you think?' Alex had tried to make his tone casual but Amber saw through him.

'Wow — your first date in how long?' she asked.

'I don't know. There's been a few,' Alex said, but he knew Amber and his whole family had noticed that he never dated any girl more than a few times before they disappeared off the scene.

'And Christina. Hmm.' Amber looked at her brother quizzically.

'What's that supposed to mean?' Alex

said, giving her a light punch on the arm.

'Ouch. She just doesn't seem your type, that's all.'

'My type? What exactly is my type supposed to be?' Alex asked.

'Well, I know I was really young but I can remember Jenna you know,' Amber said.

The sound of Jenna's name gave Alex the usual feeling in the pit of his stomach. Yes, he thought. If he had a type, Jenna was it.

But he couldn't spend the rest of his life thinking about the one that got away. If he was going to have any chance at happiness he had to go out looking for it.

He'd already wasted enough years missing someone who had become more like a fantasy than a real woman.

He'd taken Christina to see a film the following week and they'd fallen into a routine of going out together whenever they could both get time off from the hotel.

Alex knew everyone, especially Christina, was expecting them to marry or at least move in together but he'd always been the one to hold back. A conversation with Christina's father in the early days had narrowed the options down.

'So you're dating my little girl,' Bernie Mitchell had said to Alex one day when they bumped into each other in the hotel restaurant.

'Yes, sir,' Alex said, thinking 'little girl' was an odd way to refer to a woman in her twenties. Bernie came towards him until their faces were just inches apart.

'Listen to me,' he said. 'If you get any ideas about a serious relationship with my princess, you'd better make sure you make an honest woman of her, do you hear me? None of this living together rubbish.'

Alex nodded. He was left in no doubt that it would not be a good idea to cross Bernie Mitchell and his old-fashioned ideas where his daughter was concerned. And he'd stuck to that sensible pathway until this past week.

What would Bernie Mitchell's attitude be towards Alex if he ended his relationship with Christina altogether? Because that was the way Alex was starting to think.

It wasn't just because of Jenna's return to his life, though that had been the catalyst. Alex could see now that he'd carried on in the relationship with Christina because that was the easy way forward. He'd become lazy, he supposed. The feelings Jenna had stirred up had served to show him how emotionless Christina was.

He felt a pang of conscience when he realised he was just as much to blame as Christina for the state of their relationship. He'd always bowed to whatever Christina wanted if it meant he could have a quiet life. That was no basis for a future together.

Alex headed towards the suite of rooms at the hotel that Christina called home. After their discussion about

Jenna's hire car, things had been frosty between them.

Surely Christina couldn't be surprised if he now broke things off. He hadn't planned this; the idea had just jumped into his mind.

After all, it was only a short while ago when he'd broken away from Jenna because of Christina. But now he wanted to take advantage of the motivation he was feeling and split with Christina for good.

He didn't even know whether that might lead to him getting together with Jenna but he really didn't care. He wanted to free himself from what he now saw as the prison of Christina's love.

He knocked on the door and went into the sitting-room, rehearsing in his head the words he so wanted to say, but what he saw took the words from his mouth before he'd started. Christina was sitting on the sofa, a huge grin on her face and holding something he couldn't at first identify.

'Alex, what perfect timing,' she said. 'I didn't want to say anything until I'd taken the test, but now look.'

Christina held towards him the plastic stick-like object and suddenly he knew exactly what it was.

'I know we haven't planned it, my darling, but it's going to be wonderful,' Christina was saying. Alex tuned her out as she carried on. Something about when the baby was due and how she hoped it would be a boy just like him.

All Alex could think about was the future he'd been contemplating with Jenna dissolving before his eyes.

'Yes. I'm sure you're right,' he said. 'Everything's going to be wonderful.' He put an arm around Christina, wiping away a tear she probably thought was a tear of joy.

All Over Now

'Can't we meet and talk about this properly?' Bernie said. He thought if he could get the woman on to his home ground he might be able to gain an advantage.

Over the years he had been carefully stashing away not only cash but also evidence that he could use to his advantage if it became necessary at any time. Now it looked as if that time may have arrived.

'Don't be stupid,' she said. 'I can't be seen with you. And don't call me on this number again.'

She hung up the phone and missed the outraged noise that emerged on Bernie's end of the call. Nobody spoke to Bernie Mitchell like that and got away with it.

The last time he'd been called stupid, Bernie had taken great pleasure in exacting revenge. And now he'd had just about enough of being ordered around by that woman. It was time to do something he'd been contemplating for a long time.

Bernie punched another number into his phone before he could change his mind. When his lawyer answered, Bernie had his speech ready.

'I want you to set up a meeting at the District Attorney's office,' he said. 'Let's make a deal.'

Bernie was tired of the life he'd been living for the past 20 years. It had been exciting in the early days but the old saying was true — you could have too much of a good thing. And despite what the woman thought, Bernie was far from stupid. He'd seen the way things were heading for a while now.

With what he knew about the woman who thought she called the shots, Bernie was confident he could negotiate a deal that would see him walk away with a slapped wrist and a new identity.

There was only one thing that had

been holding him back until now — Christina. He couldn't walk away from his only child, no matter how old she was.

★ ★ ★

Christina was wondering what on earth she had done. A quick search on YouTube had shown her how to fake the positive pregnancy test but there was a slight flaw in her plan.

Alex might just notice when no baby appeared in eight months' time. It had been a while since the couple had shared a bed but she'd managed to convince him the test was correct.

Now, just hours later, Christina was lying awake and wishing none of the things she'd done recently were real.

It had been a stupid idea and she wished now that she hadn't done it. But she had to admit the thought of starting a family with Alex wouldn't have been the worst thing she could imagine.

They would have beautiful children,

she thought. But in a rare mood of self awareness Christina was beginning to question whether she might have gone too far.

The one thing she'd thought she was sure of was that she couldn't bear the idea of losing Alex. But was keeping him really worth all the lying and scheming?

Just before she finally dropped off to sleep Christina promised herself she would spend the next day unravelling some of the lies and covering her tracks in what she had done in an attempt to get rid of Jenna Logan. Top of the list would be telling Alex the pregnancy had been a false alarm.

★　★　★

First thing next morning Christina was supervising the breakfast service in the restaurant when Alex appeared, his face tight with anger. Christina had never seen him look this way.

'What's up?' she asked him, but

didn't give him a chance to answer. 'Come on, let's grab a coffee. I need to talk to you.' Christina was looking forward to having a clear conscience for once, as soon as she'd spoken to Alex.

'I don't want coffee,' Alex said. 'How could you?'

'How could I what?' Christina said, but an icy feeling down her spine told her what this must be about.

'I must have picked up your phone by mistake last night,' Alex said. 'Didn't notice until a text came in and I opened it. It was from Deborah.'

Deb was one of Christina's few close female friends. She was expecting her first baby and she'd been the one who came up with the idea for Christina to fake the positive pregnancy test.

There was no point discussing it with Alex. The text from Deb asking whether their trick had worked was all he'd needed to see. If Christina tried to explain now that it was all a mistake there was no way Alex would believe her.

Right at that moment Christina could have strangled Deb for sending that text. As usual she was deflecting the blame for anything that went wrong.

'I came over last night to end things between us,' Alex said and Christina flinched at his words. 'Well, after this, I'm more certain than ever. We're finished.'

Alex turned and left the restaurant and Christina waited a few moments before leaving, too, and heading to her suite.

What a Difference
a Day Makes

After his confrontation with Christina Alex had only one thought in his mind. He had to go to Jenna. He cringed as he thought about how he'd treated her over the past few days. Was there any chance Jenna would want him after he'd kept pushing her away?

His first thought when he'd seen the message from Deborah on Christina's phone had been one of anger for the way Christina had tried to trap him into continuing their relationship.

But very quickly following that another thought pushed its way in. He had gone to see Christina the previous day to end things and that message had given him the excuse to do exactly that. The main feeling overwhelming him now was a combination of relief and excitement.

He made a quick diversion to pick up a small box from his room at his parents' house. The box contained the engagement ring his grandfather had given to his grandma. It had been her dying wish that Alex, the grandson she had always doted on despite having so many of them, should give this ring to the woman he loved.

Alex knocked on Jenna's front door, his heart hammering in his chest. He was still amazed how much his life had changed since Jenna had turned up just a short time ago.

His family and friends would think he was crazy for what he was about to do.

There was no answer to his knock and Alex realised Jenna might be round the back of the house on the beach. He was right. He stood watching her while she was unaware, typing away on her laptop.

He almost hated to disturb her but then he started to feel a bit creepy standing there watching her.

'Ahem.' He coughed lightly to make her aware of his presence and she looked up, startled.

'Alex, hi,' she said with a smile that faded slightly as she was probably remembering the previous day. Alex was suddenly tongue-tied but Jenna stood and walked towards him.

'Would you like a coffee?' she said. 'I'm due a break and I was just going to have one.'

'OK,' he answered, kicking himself for losing the chance to present her with the ring in the romantic setting of the beach.

Alex was struck for the hundredth time since Jenna had come back into his life by the sense of ease he felt when they were together. They sat looking out at the view, sipping their coffee and then Alex realised he should explain why he was there.

'Jenna, I came to show you this,' he said, reaching the box out of his pocket.

Jenna's eyes widened as she opened it

and saw the beautiful solitaire diamond ring inside. Then she closed the box and gave it back to Alex, a steely look in her eyes. Alex was puzzled. What had he done wrong now?

'It's beautiful,' Jenna said. 'I'm sure Christina will love it.'

Alex put his head in his hands as he realised how dumb he'd been. He should have explained the situation before producing the ring box. He had to rescue this quickly.

'No, Jenna. Not Christina. I've ended things with her. I'll tell you all about that later. But now . . . is there any chance we could . . . '

Jenna interrupted.

'Alex, I just don't know where I am with you. One minute you're making me feel awful for wanting to kiss you, the next you're, what? Proposing to me?'

As she said the words Jenna remembered how terrible she had felt after her proposal fiasco in New York. Was that really such a short time ago?

She couldn't wish that feeling on Alex. And wasn't this exactly what she'd been dreaming of since the first day she arrived in Florida?

For once in her life maybe it was time she threw caution to the wind and did exactly what her heart told her was right.

'Say the words, Alex,' she said. 'Say them just like you did all those years ago.'

Alex knew what she meant, and he didn't need telling again.

'I'm going to marry you one day, Jenna,' he said.

'One day very soon, I hope,' Jenna answered and they fell into each other's arms.

Unexpected Invitation

Jenna was ridiculously nervous about meeting Alex's family again. She remembered half a dozen times when she was a kid, when her parents hadn't been able to get back to the hotel and Alex's mother had kindly stepped in to look after her.

For years afterwards Jenna would look back on those times and imagine she was really a part of that large, loving family, instead of an orphan who depended on the kindness of her friend's family for a secure home.

She needn't have worried. Every one of the Shepherd family went out of their way to make her welcome. Within a few minutes she was joining in with the friendly banter around the huge dining table.

Alex and Jenna had agreed it would be best to wait until after the meal to make their announcement. Jenna had decided not to wear the engagement ring until Alex had told his family about their plans.

He'd been with Christina for such a long time without getting engaged, it was likely to come as a shock after he and Jenna had only been together for days. But of course, in their hearts it had really been years.

Alex touched his knife against his glass to get everyone's attention. There had been two or three different conversations going on throughout the meal. The Shepherd house was always full of noise and love and these family gatherings were a regular thing each person around the table hated to miss.

'OK, guys, I have something to tell you,' he said. 'I mean, we have something to tell you.' He took Jenna's hand before carrying on. 'You all know things haven't worked out between me and Christina. Well, Jenna isn't to blame for that, but we are together now.'

Alex's mother grinned — she'd never made a secret of the fact she disliked Christina Mitchell. When Alex had told her about the break up it was the best news she'd heard in ages.

After a few comments about how they'd all been expecting this, the rest of the family started chatting again, unimpressed by Alex's statement. He hit the glass again, a bit louder this time.

'Hang on,' he said, smiling at Jenna. 'That's not all. I know this might seem a bit sudden but ... ' He pulled Grandma's ring out of his pocket and slid it on to Jenna's finger. 'We're getting married.'

There was a second or two of silence before the whoops and cheers began.

Jenna glanced at Mrs Shepherd to make sure the grin was still on her face and was relieved to see it was an even wider smile than before. She came round the table and hugged them both.

'When can we go dress shopping?' she asked and a tear crept from Jenna's eye as she realised the other woman was naturally stepping into the role her own mother would have relished.

'Whenever you like,' Jenna said.

She was so happy when Alex dropped her off at home she wanted to hug the feeling to her and never let it go. The only slight disappointment was that Alex had to leave so he could be up early.

He was going out of town for a couple of days. Something to do with the dive school, though Jenna wasn't sure exactly what. She was happy to see him enthusiastic about his plans for the place. Jenna planned to get on with some writing while he was gone. But the best-laid plans . . .

⋆ ⋆ ⋆

Early the next morning the doorbell rang and Jenna hurried downstairs to answer it, wrapping her new robe around her as she went. Her cupboards and drawers were now full of the new clothes she'd ordered the day she moved in.

Of all the people she might have guessed would be on her doorstep this was the last one. Christina Mitchell. But there was something different about her — she looked almost friendly. Jenna wasn't sure what to do. The last thing she felt like doing was inviting Christina into her new home.

'Can I come in?' Christina asked.

Politeness won out and Jenna stood to one side then followed Christina down the hall to the kitchen. Five minutes later the two women were sitting with cups of coffee at the kitchen table.

Politeness had forced Jenna into this uncomfortable situation but she was determined not to feel obliged to make small talk.

'I'm sorry,' Christina said.

'For what?' Jenna said. Although she'd suspected Christina was behind the damage to her rental car the other day, there was no proof so she wanted to hear Christina say the words.

'For how I've treated you since you arrived,' Christina said. 'I've done a lot of thinking these past few days and I realise I've behaved like an idiot. I know everyone thinks I'm a spoilt brat who depends on her daddy for everything. But I've had to face up to some harsh facts since Alex . . . ended things. I'm hoping you'll let me make it up to you.'

'How?' Jenna said, but what she was really thinking was why? In Christina's place all she'd want to do would be to lick her wounds and move on.

'I heard your news,' Christina said. 'About the engagement.' The last word came out on something that could have been a sob but Christina turned it into a cough. 'I'd like to show you there's no hard feelings,' she continued. 'Come and be my guest at the hotel spa today. On me.'

Jenna didn't know what to say. Half her brain was wondering how Christina had heard about the engagement so quickly and the other half was thinking about her endless to-do list.

She'd promised herself to work on the blog all day but it seemed so unfriendly to turn down Christina's generous offer. And the offer was very tempting. It was ages since Jenna had enjoyed a spa day and the chance to relax and let the world go by was too good to miss.

'OK,' she said. 'Give me ten minutes to get dressed.'

Jenna missed the gleam in Christina's eye as she smiled to herself and carried on sipping her coffee. It had been much easier than she'd expected to persuade Jenna to come with her.

She'd been doing so well for a day or two, sticking to her resolution. Then Deb had told her what all her other friends hadn't dared to mention. No sooner had Alex finished with her than he was engaged to Jenna Logan.

Christina's hatred of Jenna and her determination to get rid of her had flared up with a vengeance.

A Matter of Life or Death

Within an hour they were at the hotel, about to go into the sauna, when Christina's phone rang as she was stashing it in a locker.

She'd explained to Jenna that they'd had reports of phones being damaged in the hot steam so they'd both been packing their belongings into lockers.

'I'm sorry,' she said when she saw who was calling. 'I really have to take this. I'll be back in five minutes, you go ahead.'

Jenna went into the room that was more of a small cabin. She adjusted the sauna controls and started to make herself comfortable.

As she sat down she thought she saw a fleeting movement through the circular window in the cabin door. Probably just another spa client, she thought.

As she began to relax, Jenna's thoughts drifted back over the past few days and she found herself trying to rationalise all the things that had happened.

It would be far more comforting to think the events were mere coincidences or down to bad luck rather than that there was someone out to get her.

Minutes passed and Jenna was wondering why Christina hadn't returned and also why it had become so hot so quickly. She stood and went to the control dial. The temperature was reading much higher than she'd set but the dial wouldn't move.

A vague feeling of unease started to come over her. She tried the door handle but it was stuck. She rattled it a few times then started to bang hard on the door and shout for help.

It was so hot now Jenna was worried she might pass out. She didn't know what to do. Unless Christina came back soon, Jenna realised, this could be life threatening.

Then a terrible thought struck her.

Despite all her earlier musing about coincidence and bad luck, what if Christina had set this up deliberately? Then she wouldn't be coming back at all.

* ★ ★ ★

Alex had set off early to reach Tampa in time for the business seminar he was booked on. As he drove over the Sunshine Skyway bridge the morning sun was shimmering on the sea at either side.

He'd decided it was time to start taking the dive school seriously — maybe expand it to a few more beaches — and he wanted to learn how to run things properly.

Although he knew Jenna was pleased to see him concentrating on the business, he hadn't told her about the course because he was planning to tell her all about his plans when he felt more confident that he knew what he was doing.

Now he was glad he hadn't mentioned it. He'd only gone and turned up on the wrong week, hadn't he? How was he ever going to run a successful business if he couldn't even use a calendar?

He was on his way back to St Pete and wondering whether to drop in at Jenna's or just go and do some work at the hotel.

In the end he decided he was too embarrassed by his mistake to face Jenna. He went to the hotel, planning to change into shorts and T-shirt then keep himself busy.

Alex had a locker full of clean shorts and shirts that he kept down in the spa for when he'd been doing some particularly messy jobs and needed to shower and change without going home.

As he headed to the locker room he heard a strange banging noise and soon realised it was coming from one of the saunas. Seconds later he'd wrenched open the door and was horrified to see

Jenna lying on the floor wrapped in a fluffy white towel.

'Jenna!' he shouted, dragging her from the steam filled cabin, then quickly dialling 911 on his phone.

What Does the Future Hold?

Alex had been waiting outside the hospital room for an hour by the time anyone came out to let him know what was happening. It was the longest hour of his life as he waited to find out how seriously ill Jenna was. He'd had to be economical with the truth so the staff would treat him as her next of kin.

When a nurse had asked him if he was a close relative, he simply hadn't denied it and he'd later heard her refer to him as the patient's brother. If the mistake was going to allow him in to see her Alex decided he wouldn't correct it.

'Jenna's going to be OK,' the nurse told him at last. 'But she'll have to stay here overnight so we can keep an eye on her. Heat exhaustion can be very serious.'

Alex felt like he could breathe again for the first time since he'd found Jenna on that floor.

'Thank you,' he said. 'Can I see her?'

'Just for a few minutes. She needs some rest.'

Alex slipped into the room. The sight of Jenna lying on the hospital bed with her eyes closed made him thankful he'd had to return from Tampa.

If he hadn't, the chances were that Jenna would be dead now. The rest of the spa had been deserted so there had been nobody to hear her banging on the door and calling for help.

If he'd stayed longer in the city or decided not to come into the hotel he dreaded to think what might have happened. He refused to let himself carry on thinking along those lines.

'Jenna,' he whispered and took hold of her hand, squeezing it gently. 'Sorry,' he said when she opened her eyes. 'Were you sleeping?'

'No, just resting my eyes,' Jenna croaked. The heat and her screams for help that went unheard had left her throat feeling raw and painful.

'Shush,' Alex said. 'Rest your voice, too. We don't need to talk. I just wanted to be with you.'

Jenna smiled and closed her eyes again. A few minutes later the nurse popped her head around the door and Alex thought she was going to tell him to leave but that wasn't it.

'There's a police officer here to speak to Jenna,' she said, looking at Alex strangely. It took him a moment to realise he was sitting closer and holding hands tighter than a brother probably would.

'Do you think she's up to being interviewed?' he asked.

'Doctor says it's fine,' the nurse said and disappeared.

Alex helped Jenna take a drink of water while they waited for the police officer.

'I don't understand why it's a police

matter,' Alex said. 'Surely it was just a faulty sauna control.'

'But what about the door?' Jenna said, her voice a little stronger now.

'What about it? I got in to rescue you with no problem.'

'But I couldn't open it from inside. I think someone had tampered with the handle. And the sauna control. That's what I told the doctors and they must have called the police. What's the matter?'

Alex was thinking hard. There was only one person who would want to cause harm to Jenna and who was crazy enough to actually do it.

'I've been trying to work out why you were there,' he said. They hadn't had chance to talk to each other between Alex rescuing her and now. 'Was it Christina's idea for you to come to the spa?'

Jenna nodded.

'OK,' Alex continued. 'Well, don't expect the police department to help. You wouldn't believe the number of people who've come into conflict with the Mitchells over the years and ended up with no help from the police.'

'Christina's father pays off the police?' Jenna asked, wide eyed.

'I can't prove it but anyone in town would tell you the same,' Alex said.

★   ★   ★

Half an hour later Jenna was forced to admit it looked as if Alex was right. The uniformed police officer who had come to interview Jenna didn't even take any notes.

He told her it looked like what had happened was an unfortunate accident. She might want to take civil action against the hotel but there was no evidence of anything criminal.

'There won't be,' Alex said once the officer had left. 'By now the sauna will have been repaired and there'll be no way of knowing what happened.' He also knew Bernie Mitchell's lawyer would be able to make it look like

Jenna's fault if she dared take them to court.

'So I'm supposed to just let Christina get away with it? Again?' Jenna said.

'Again?' Alex asked, then remembered the rental car brakes. It really was starting to look like Christina had a deadly vendetta against Jenna. It was up to him to keep Jenna safe.

'Listen,' he said. 'How would you feel if I moved into your new place?'

Wow, Jenna thought. Every cloud really does have a silver lining. She hadn't considered it but the idea immediately grew on her.

The whole idea of finding somewhere to rent had been to have somewhere she could be alone, but she would feel much safer with Alex around. Plus it would really annoy Christina, which was a bonus.

Immediately after that thought, Jenna started to wonder what further ways to harm her Christina might come up with if she was so provoked.

'I'll move into the spare room until

our wedding, if you like,' Alex said and Jenna wondered if it was possible for him to be any more lovable.

'We'll see,' she said, wincing as Alex kissed her on lips that were starting to blister. Exhaustion washed over Jenna and she started to fall asleep. Alex crept from the room.

His first instinct was to go back to the hotel and confront Christina with what she'd done, but when had that ever done any good?

Instead he went home and packed enough clothes for a week or so. He'd picked up Jenna's bag at the spa so he had a door key and let himself into her house. Ten minutes later he'd unpacked his things and put them away in the spare room.

Alex didn't need to be anywhere. He'd taken two days off from the hotel for the mistaken business seminar and also closed the dive school for the rest of the week.

Although he'd gone back to the hotel earlier with the intention of working, now he couldn't think of anything he wanted to do less. This was the first chance he'd had in a long time to spend some time alone just thinking about life in general.

His whole world had been turned upside down that day when Jenna turned up in the hotel reception. He realised now that up to that moment he had been trundling along on autopilot.

How had he ever ended up in a relationship with Christina Mitchell? And what repercussions would there be now he'd ended it?

It looked as though Christina had turned her heartbreak or disappointment into a quest for revenge against Jenna. But what about Bernie Mitchell? Alex was surprised he hadn't yet become aware of Bernie's displeasure at someone hurting his daughter. His princess. Alex knew he would have to be very wary for a while.

Key to the Problem

When Bernie Mitchell learned of the incident at the hotel spa he was angry. Very angry. He knew straight away who was behind it and why.

As soon as Christina had told him about Alex Shepherd's new girlfriend he'd warned her. He couldn't be completely truthful with his daughter about why she had to step back from any involvement with Jenna Logan so he turned the situation around.

'Do not let this affect the business,' he'd said. Of course, Christina hadn't understood. And now it looked like she'd ignored him and not even his princess was allowed to do that.

'I'm sorry, Daddy,' Christina said when he confronted her. As usual, seeing Christina upset chipped away at Bernie's determination to be strict with her.

Whatever punishment or sanctions he'd thought about were replaced by a good telling off and orders not to ignore him again. Bernie even said she could choose the restaurant for their next monthly meeting which was a first.

'But in future, princess,' he said, 'make sure anything reckless like this takes place well away from the hotel or any other of my businesses. You think people are going to be queuing up to use a spa where something like this has happened?'

'No, Daddy, you're right, of course,' Christina said, keeping up the dutiful daughter act. Her father was starting to annoy her now, pointing out her mistake so bluntly, but she had the sense to assure him she was taking his advice to heart.

Neither of the Mitchells was aware of the rumours flying around Bernie's staff.

Most people were willing to believe that the incident with the sauna was an unfortunate accident but they were far more interested in something else. It was unheard of for Bernie to leave alone someone who had disrespected his family.

Alex Shepherd had humiliated Bernie Mitchell's daughter by dumping her and getting engaged to someone else immediately. Was the boss going soft? If so, there were plenty of people who might fancy their chances of getting one over on him.

★   ★   ★

Alex had brought in Jenna's laptop when he came to visit that evening. He'd also brought a box of chocolates for the nurse he'd spoken to earlier, who was just going off shift as he arrived.

A quick apology for his deception when pretending to be Jenna's brother was in order, Alex had decided. It was looking as though Jenna would have to stay here another night and he couldn't stand the thought of having to keep up the pretence. The nurse laughed it off. After all, she dealt with far more serious matters most of the time.

Jenna was keen to get on with some work.

'That's the great thing about technology,' she said to Alex as she powered up the laptop. 'I can work pretty much anywhere.'

Her words reminded Alex he was due back at work at the hotel the next day. Plenty of time to worry about that later, though, he decided.

'Do you mind if I keep you company while you work?' he said.

'Not at all,' Jenna said. She was relishing the chance to spend some time alone with Alex, even if it was in a hospital room.

As she opened her blog file, though, she started to feel a little self-conscious. For the first time she realised she was almost always alone when she wrote. Well, it wasn't as if Alex was going to try to read over her shoulder.

Half an hour later Jenna closed the laptop.

'That's enough for now,' she said. 'I didn't realise how tired I still was.'

They decided to watch some trashy TV for a while, enjoying the opportunity to chill out together, only disturbed by the occasional visits from nurses or the meal trolley. Alex dashed out to pick up a sandwich so he could join Jenna having lunch.

'Are you sure you don't have anything better to do?' Jenna asked when they'd both finished eating. Alex looked her in the eye. When would she understand there would never be anything better for him to do than spend time with her? he wondered.

'I'm happy here for now,' he said, 'but don't let me stop you working. I'll just keep watching 'Storage Hunters' or whatever's on next.'

Jenna laughed as she signed back on to her laptop and opened her e-mails. She saw the message from Nonnie straight away and it dawned on her that here was her chance to get someone else's perspective.

'Alex, read this,' she said, turning the screen round.

Alex read the brief message, raising his eyebrows as the words sank in.

'Dear Jenna, My fiancé's ex just tried to kill me. I've told the police but they don't believe me. What should I do?'

'What the . . . ' Alex started but Jenna interrupted.

'I literally just finished typing up some notes about what happened at the spa,' she said. 'It's not on my blog, just in another document. It's not the first time it's happened, either. I haven't told you because I hoped it would have stopped by now. But look.' She scrolled through the messages she'd managed to copy and save. 'There were more but they all disappear as soon as I've closed my e-mails down.'

'Weird,' Alex said, thinking rapidly. 'Listen, I'm no computer expert but I do know one. My kid brother, Adam, knows all about this sort of stuff. If you can do without your laptop for a few hours I'll see if he can help.'

★   ★   ★

Adam Shepherd was bored that afternoon so he jumped at the chance to see what was up with Jenna's laptop, especially when Alex said there would be a few dollars in it. It only took him an hour to get to the bottom of the mystery.

'Keystroke logging software,' he announced, handing the laptop back to Alex. 'I've wiped it off without affecting any of Jenna's files. Whoever installed the software will have been able to replicate anything Jenna typed on that laptop.'

'Is there any way of finding out how this was done? It's really been messing with Jenna's head,' Alex said, then laughed at the expression on his brother's face. He already knew but he was waiting for Alex to offer more of a reward. He nodded. 'Go on, tell me.'

165

'Well, I'm not sure about the first couple of e-mails because they were sent before the software was installed and the first one was immediately deleted.

'But it looks as though this person used that first message to send the code to Jenna's laptop which would install the keystroke logging program. Then all they had to do was sit back and monitor what Jenna was typing.

'They could also have monitored Jenna's passwords and they would've been able to access any of her files and e-mails.'

Alex swapped the computer for a couple of banknotes and punched his brother's arm on the way out of the room.

'Thanks, kid,' he shouted as he left the house. He'd only understood about half of what Adam had told him but that was enough.

Will Jenna Learn the Truth?

Jenna had almost missed the e-mail in amongst a lot of spam and she read it twice before she was convinced it was genuine and it stirred up memories of things that she was starting to wish would just stay in the past.

But once the implications of the message sank in fully she realised she couldn't pretend it wasn't real. It hinted that there was more to what had happened to her parents than she had been told and that it was a very serious matter.

The conclusion Jenna couldn't avoid was that there was something sinister about the accident.

Jenna still couldn't get her head around all that had happened in such a short time. Everything she'd believed about her family, her past and her future was up in the air.

Could it really be true about her parents' accident being suspicious? Well, she would soon find out.

Someone from the FBI had flown down to Florida to meet with Jenna. They wouldn't do that if there wasn't at least a grain of truth in the information contained in the e-mail. In the next hour she would find out the truth at last.

The meeting was arranged for 11 o'clock at the police headquarters in town and Jenna arrived early. She'd decided not to tell Alex about it — he was bound to say he didn't think she was up to it so soon after getting out of the hospital.

But even though she'd been enjoying Alex's protectiveness she felt it was time now to start doing things by herself sometimes.

Finally she was ushered into the meeting room and a tall, thin woman in a smart business suit stood to greet her.

'Ms Logan, I'm Olivia Harris, would you like to see my identification?'

'No, thank you.' Jenna didn't see the point of insisting on seeing the woman's ID. They would hardly have allowed her to host a meeting in the police headquarters if she was an imposter.

Jenna sat on the chair Olivia Harris had placed close to her own. There was probably some deep psychological reason for the way she'd placed them but Jenna couldn't be bothered wondering about it at the moment.

'OK, Ms Logan . . . '

'Jenna, please,' Jenna interrupted. This meeting was going to be hard enough without having to be addressed so formally all the way through.

'Jenna. Thank you. Now, what I'm about to tell you may come as a shock so please ask me to stop if you need to. Are you sure you wouldn't like to have someone here with you?'

'No, it's fine.' There was only Alex and, as she'd been thinking earlier, she knew he would support her afterwards. For now there was no need to ask him to give up his time when she knew the dive school was fully booked.

She wished Olivia Harris would get on with it but knew she had to be patient and allow her to go at her own speed. And Jenna needed to try and stop drifting back in time to the last time she'd seen her parents.

Dangerous Mission

Paul and Karen Logan left the apartment with heavy hearts. Although they both knew they were right to have decided that Jenna must stay behind so she didn't miss school, that wasn't the only reason their daughter was excluded from this trip.

'She'll be safe here, that's the main thing,' Paul said, looking at his wife's troubled face.

'I just wish there was another way to deal with all this,' Karen said. She didn't need to define what she meant by 'all this'.

They'd both been at the meeting the previous day when their supervisor, Olivia Harris, had brought them up to date with developments on the case they were working on.

It was the news they'd been waiting for. It looked as though years of work by a large team of undercover agents was about to come to fruition.

The Logans, as special prosecutors, had been involved from day one and, although they worked on other cases alongside, this was the one that had taken up most of their attention.

It had soon become clear that they would have to travel to Florida immediately. They were in possession of knowledge that only they and their supervisor had shared. Without them, the teams of investigators each held just a small part of the puzzle.

When the Logans arrived they would bring everything together and bring down a crime ring that had dominated the state and large parts of the rest of the country for decades. Although the New York office was in charge of the overall investigation it looked as though things were finally going to come to a head in Florida.

'Looks like our anniversary dinner's off,' Karen said miserably as they left the office. The couple had always made a point of celebrating the anniversary of the happiest day of their lives.

'We'll just about have time to pack and explain to Jenna that she'll have to stay at Tiffany's . . . '

'Don't be so defeatist,' Paul said. 'And don't underestimate your husband.'

Karen had no idea what he meant until she opened the dining-room door at the apartment.

The table was set for two, candles and all, and their daughter was standing by the door dressed like a silver-service waitress. She couldn't keep up the act for long and they all dissolved into laughter.

'Dad called and gave me my instructions an hour ago,' Jenna said. 'I think I've done pretty well in that time, don't you?'

Jenna left her parents to it once she'd served them the dinner she'd ordered in from the local Chinese restaurant. She had plenty of studying to do before packing for a few days at her best friend's place.

When Dad had let slip that he and her mother were off to Florida without her she'd been dismayed at first but then she realised it was the first time her parents had trusted her to be out of their sight for so long. Maybe they were finally realising she was growing up.

Most of Jenna's friends were allowed much more freedom than she had and sometimes it really got on her nerves. But deep down she knew her parents were only trying to keep her safe and happy.

Paul could see Karen relaxing for the first time in weeks as she took a few sips of the crisp white wine Jenna had placed in an ice bucket on the table. Not for the first time he wondered why they both still did this crazily stressful job.

Well, not for much longer, he thought, clinking his glass against his wife's. Once this case was finished Paul planned to talk to Karen about early retirement or at least a career change to something less risky.

'Happy anniversary, my darling,' he said.

'And to you,' Karen said. 'How can it possibly be twenty years?' They both laughed.

The couple had met in law school. Hardly love at first sight — Paul had been forced to sit next to Karen at their first lecture when he arrived late and that was the only seat left.

They'd barely noticed each other until the following term when a mutual friend had organised a surprise party for a roommate.

Embarrassingly, Karen and Paul were the only two people who turned up and they endured awkward small talk for an hour before they both made their excuses pleading the need to study for an exam the next day.

Instead they had adjourned to the nearest bar and ended up with the staff clearing up around them and pointedly looking at their watches.

After that they were inseparable.

They'd learned a lesson when they both missed out on their usual top grades in the exam the day after that awful party. In future they became known as the geekiest couple in town, spending their evenings studying together and only socialising during holidays.

It was inevitable that Paul and Karen would marry and they did so as soon as they'd graduated from law school, joint top of their class.

When they were accepted together on to the career path that would lead to becoming special prosecutors it seemed like fate.

If they'd thought law school was tough, the next few years made that look like a holiday camp but Paul and Karen thrived on the hard work. And as well as working hard they played hard, making up for their years of staying in with their books.

After struggling financially as students they were enjoying the chance to take holidays in exotic places and they built up a small but close group of friends. Life was perfect.

At least it was for the first few years. Then the perfect Logans who planned every part of their lives were suddenly thrown a curve ball.

'I'm late,' Karen said.

'No, I don't think so,' Paul said, looking at his watch. 'We said twelve and it's dead on.'

Karen sighed. For a supposedly super-intelligent lawyer her husband could be very dumb at times.

'I said I'm late. I didn't mean the time. I meant . . . oh, come on, Paul, you know. I think I'm pregnant.'

Paul looked exactly as stunned as Karen herself had looked when it dawned on her. but after the initial shock, she'd started to wonder if it would be such a bad thing. Paul needed a little more convincing.

'Kids weren't in the plan, Karen. We talked about this. Our jobs are too all-consuming. It wouldn't be fair on a child.'

Karen knew he was right — that had

been the plan. But all of a sudden the plan didn't seem so important.

'I'll give up work,' she said, surprising herself as much as Paul. As soon as the words were out of her mouth she was questioning them but after debating for hours it seemed it would be the only option.

As soon as she informed her work supervisor she was taken off any active case investigations and felt like she was tied to her desk. She spent most of her pregnancy wondering what on earth she was letting herself in for.

Her whole education and ambitions had been geared to this career she loved and now she felt like it was disappearing down the drain.

But the moment Jenna was born Karen knew she had done the right thing. This time it really was love at first sight.

From that first day until Jenna started school, mother and daughter were rarely apart. If she felt any regret as she watched Paul forge ahead in his career she didn't show it. But they'd discussed it and Jenna starting school seemed the perfect time for Karen to return to work.

It was several years before she caught up enough to work as a team with Paul again and that's when they were assigned to the case that would bring them to Florida each year.

Now the adult Logans were on their way to the airport and it was time to switch mode from anxious parents to dedicated professionals.

Karen checked for the tenth time that she had the laptop containing the key codes to the files that would make sense of the whole investigation. Their supervisor had told them not to make contact with her until the case was closed. They interpreted this, correctly, to mean there was a concern about leaks in the investigation.

By the time they landed, the couple were well and truly back in work mode, though being back in Florida always made Karen nostalgic. This trip should be our final one on this case, she thought.

She remembered all those other times when they had brought Jenna with them and she'd enjoyed the beach holiday with her friend while they spent some time working, unbeknown to their daughter.

Had they been endangering her? No, they'd risk assessed the situation thoroughly many times. And what if, after this trip, their daughter could no longer visit her friend, Alex? Well, there would be nothing stopping the Logans holidaying here as usual, would there?

The more Karen thought about it, she was able to picture a future free of the stress of this case that had been hanging over them for years. The possibilities for their small family were endless.

Lying Low

Paul and Karen picked up an unremarkable hire car and headed straight to their base for the next few days.

They'd decided not to stay at their usual hotel at St Pete. It wasn't because of any suspicion that the staff there were involved in what they were investigating. They'd got to know the family who owned the place over the years and would have vouched for any of them.

No, the reason they were staying at a resort further up the coast at Clearwater was because they didn't want to risk the safety of their St Pete friends.

They were using an apartment they'd set up as a safe house years ago. Even their supervisor, Olivia Harris, was in the dark on this one. Again, that wasn't due to any suspicion about Olivia. It was just a feeling that Karen had told Paul about.

'And what's the first lesson we learned when we signed up to this job?' her husband had said when she mentioned it. 'Always be prepared and always follow your instincts.'

Neither of them realised that, on this occasion, their instincts might have let them down. From the moment they'd left the airport they had been followed and the apartment was no longer the safe house it was intended to be.

Karen had been relieved he hadn't laughed off her worries. They'd never needed to use the safe apartment before but it had always been there just in case.

Even she couldn't put her finger on why she hadn't wanted to stay at the official accommodation that had been arranged for them. Within a couple of hours the apartment looked like a computer hacker's paradise as the Logans set up the equipment they would need.

'Time to go out and get some supplies,' Paul said. 'We might be here for some time.'

Although it was only a matter of hours since they'd been enjoying their romantic anniversary meal, Karen felt as if it was a lifetime ago.

They quickly stocked up on ready meals and other essentials and hurried back to the apartment. It would be foolish to risk being seen at this stage and it could blow the whole investigation apart.

They needed to lie low until the next day when a meeting had been arranged that could lead to the showdown they were expecting.

Karen found she was getting ahead of herself, envisaging the end of the operation when they could return home to their beloved daughter. It was time to put those thoughts aside and concentrate on the job they'd come here to do.

Dinner that evening was a far cry from the romantic meal of the night before.

Karen chuckled as she poured them each a glass of fruit juice. No alcohol allowed whilst on assignment was one of the rules that had served them well over the years. You never knew when you'd have to drive at a moment's notice.

The evening stretched ahead of them, all preparations completed and nothing to do other than choose between cable TV and an early night. They chose the latter, falling into each other's arms like newly-weds rather than a couple who had just celebrated 20 years of marriage.

Last Wish

Next morning Paul and Karen were up at the crack of dawn and ready to leave for their meeting. Even allowing for rush hour traffic it was far too soon so they sat around watching the clock. Karen suggested coffee but Paul shook his head.

'I'm wound up enough. Caffeine would not help at this point,' he said.

Karen was relieved he had admitted to being as nervous as she herself felt. It was an unusual feeling for both of them. Usually they were calm and cool in all their professional dealings.

'It must be the thought of all the people and all the time that's gone into this,' she said and Paul agreed. He looked at his wife and seemed to be struggling with whether to say his next words.

'I've been thinking about this for a

while,' he finally said. 'After this case I definitely want to look into leaving the organisation and finding something a little less, er, demanding.'

Karen considered his words. She'd been thinking along the same lines for a while but she was still surprised Paul felt this way. She'd always thought he would have to be dragged kicking and screaming from his office when his time came to retire. A smile spread slowly across her features.

'You have no idea how happy I am to hear you say that,' she said, grabbing Paul's hand and kissing it. And that was it. Their future decided. Now all they had to do was go out and finish this job.

As he drove the rental car out of the parking space in front of the building Paul became aware of a vehicle 50 yards behind doing the same manoeuvre. Of course it could just be coincidence that they'd pulled into traffic at the same time as that other car — but maybe it wasn't.

He kept an eye on it in the rear view

mirror for the first few minutes of their journey but eventually the other driver turned right at a traffic signal and Paul relaxed.

They were driving towards the area of the coast they were more familiar with now. All those summers when they'd been here doing background investigation work meant they knew the place almost as well as where they lived in New York.

It took a few moments for Paul to realise that other car, or one identical to it, was on their tail again. He decided not to say anything to Karen. No point worrying her unless he was certain there was a problem. The next stretch of road contained several hairpin bends and he needed to concentrate.

They never made it past that stretch of hairpin bends. The emergency services who responded to the accident report located black skid marks leading to a broken crash barrier.

The Logans' rental car had plunged over the edge of the road and though the rescue crews battled heroically to get to the casualties it was clear, when they were finally reached, they had died instantly.

Stunning Revelations

Olivia Harris took a deep breath, obviously ready to start at last.

'Let's start with your parents' accident. As you know, there's been a complete reinvestigation and it's shown up some problems with the original case. Their deaths should not have been ruled accidental. The new investigation may well lead to charges related to murder or at least manslaughter.'

Jenna gasped. She'd been expecting that news but it still hit her hard.

'Now,' Olivia continued, 'let's move on to the reason they were in the area at that time. As you know, they were called away from New York at short notice.'

Jenna nodded but didn't want to interrupt the other woman now she was in full flow.

'If I'm right in assuming you were

unaware of the reason they were here,' Olivia said, 'then this next part will come as a shock. Jenna, your mother and father worked for the FBI.'

'But . . . ' Jenna couldn't resist interrupting after all. 'But they were both lawyers. They worked for clients, not for law enforcement.'

'They were lawyers, but they were what's known as special prosecutors. They worked for the organisation on high-profile cases, sometimes lasting for years and sometimes under cover and highly confidential.' She let this sink in for a moment, knowing Jenna would have a hundred questions buzzing round her head.

'If the case they were working on for years was based around here,' Jenna said slowly, as the implications began to hit her, 'does that mean when we were on holiday here they were actually working?'

Thinking back, it made sense of all the times she'd been left at a loose end while her parents were off doing their own thing. At the time she'd hardly given them a second thought — she was just happy to be with Alex.

'They were dedicated to their work,' Olivia said. 'But they were also dedicated to you and making sure you had holidays and trips just like any of your school friends. They would have done a risk assessment before they brought you here to make sure it was safe.

'That last time they must have decided it was too dangerous for you to accompany them. And they were right.'

'So all these years when I've been feeling guilty because I wasn't with them . . . ' Jenna said.

'You have nothing whatsoever to feel guilty about. They were doing the jobs they loved and it was their decision to leave you in New York,' Olivia said. 'They were a huge loss to our organisation and to the country. You can be proud of them.'

'Oh, I am. I always have been but now I know the truth I'm even more proud.'

Jenna felt tears starting to threaten but she was determined not to let them out. She sat bolt upright as a thought hit her for the first time.

'Who killed them?'

'As I said earlier there are likely to be charges brought,' Olivia said, 'but at this moment I can't name any names. We're sure we have the people who killed them in custody, but we're still trying to locate the people who ordered their murder.'

'Ordered their murder?' Jenna repeated. 'As in a contract killing? As in hiring hit men?'

''It's complicated, Jenna. The people they were investigating are involved in many types of crime. Over the years, using your parents' background work, we've managed to take several of them out of circulation.

'You won't have read about it in the papers because we've still been targeting the people at the top. And we're close now. I promise you.'

Jenna could tell from Olivia's tone of

voice that she was starting to bring the meeting to a close. She tried to think of all the questions she'd thought about overnight but they'd all been eclipsed by Olivia's revelations.

'Thank you for coming all this way to speak to me,' Jenna said, standing and shaking hands with Olivia Harris.

Olivia smiled.

'Well, I have to admit I needed to come here for a few other reasons,' she said. 'But my first priority was speaking to you and giving you a long overdue explanation.'

* * *

As Jenna walked away from the building she thought about Olivia's last words. Should she be angry that she'd been kept in the dark all these years?

She couldn't find it in herself to be angry at her parents, who only kept their true occupations from her to keep her safe. She was sure that if they'd still been alive they would have told her eventually. Maybe once she left school or at some other life milestone.

She wondered if her uncle was in the know. If he was, then she felt he should have told her once she was old enough to understand. But what good would it have done?

No, she decided, she had been better off in ignorance until now. It was only now that the FBI was on the verge of completing the work started by Karen and Paul Logan. The knowledge would have been of no use to Jenna beforehand.

It was a little frustrating that she wasn't allowed to know all the details of the new investigation into her parents' deaths, but again what would she have been able to do with the knowledge? Become some sort of vigilante taking out the heads of the local organised crime gangs? She couldn't visualise herself as a kind of avenging angel.

She would put what she had learned to the back of her mind and get on with her life.

Glancing at her watch, Jenna saw it was just coming up to the time Alex would have finished for the morning. Maybe she'd be able to join him for lunch at the beach bar. Life was good.

A thought flitted through her mind but was gone again before she'd seriously considered it. How had Olivia Harris known she was here or known her contact details to arrange the meeting?

Olivia Harris watched from the window as Jenna Logan left the building. She analysed how she was feeling as she watched this woman walk away. Any twinges of conscience? No. Olivia had to admit she didn't really know the meaning of the word.

Meeting with Jenna had simply been a way of justifying travelling to Florida at this time. And now she was here it was time to get on with what she had really come for. She reached her phone from her bag. Her other phone, that is. The one she saved for the darker side of her life.

'It's done. I've seen her,' she said when her call was answered. Whatever the person on the other end of the call said it seemed to amuse Olivia. 'Yes, I could certainly tell whose daughter she is. I'll be with you in an hour.'

Just time to tidy up a couple of other loose ends, she thought as she put the phone away.

Kidnapped!

For ever afterwards Jenna would wonder how on earth she had allowed what happened next to happen. She'd lived in New York all her life; she should be streetwise. But since she'd been back in Florida Jenna seemed to have lost her natural awareness of the dangers around her.

So when the black pickup truck crawled to a halt beside her as she was waiting to cross the road she didn't think twice about it. And when the driver put his window down and shouted her name it still didn't seem odd to her.

Only when a figure dressed in jeans and a hoodie jumped out of the passenger side and bundled her into the truck with him did she realise the danger.

'What are you doing? Let me go!' she

shouted. After that everything went black. It was only much later that she realised she'd been injected with a sedative.

She woke in a dark, cool, musty-smelling room that she soon figured out was a garage. Her head was swimming but the first definite thought that crossed her mind was this was another attempt by Christina Mitchell to get rid of her.

Tampering with the rental car hadn't worked because Alex had been there to save Jenna. The same thing had happened at the spa with the sauna incident. But how would Alex save her this time?

From what she could remember there hadn't been any people nearby on the street when she was forced into the pickup truck. With no witnesses it would be as if she had simply vanished into thin air.

Jenna was trying her very best not to sink into despair in this situation but she had no idea where she was or what was going to happen to her next.

Surely if Christina wanted her dead it would have happened by now. But what if she wanted Jenna to suffer first? Jenna put a stop to those sort of thoughts straight away and started looking for a way out of the garage.

They hadn't tied her up so they must have been pretty sure there was no way for her to escape. They hadn't left her any food or water. Did that mean they were simply going to leave her there to die of thirst?

Stop it! she told herself. She patted her pocket, hoping against hope that they hadn't found her phone but it was no use. Of course they had searched her before leaving her.

The only thing Jenna still had that was any comfort to her was the watch she always wore, the one her parents had given her for her sixteenth birthday. It kept perfect time and displayed the date.

She tried not to think of it as a way of counting down her final hours. At least she'd be able to keep track of how long she'd been here.

She had to assume she'd only been unconscious for a few hours at the most and she could work out the time between her meeting with Olivia Harris and the time her watch now showed. Concentrating on that would keep her from her earlier despairing thoughts.

It was evening now and Alex would surely be getting concerned about her. Would he report her missing or assume she had gone off alone, maybe to meet someone, without telling him?

For the next few minutes, Jenna put all her mental energy into willing Alex to report her to the police as missing. Then she realised that even if he did, the police probably wouldn't do anything about it for at least 24 hours.

Then she remembered what Alex had told her about most of the town's police being paid off by the Mitchells. It seemed as if every time she had a positive thought a negative one came rushing straight in after.

Despite her best intentions to stay awake and alert Jenna gave in to sleep eventually. When she woke up on the concrete floor it took her a few moments to remember what had happened.

As she had known she would be, Jenna was glad of the watch that helped her work out whether it was day or night and how long she had been cooped up. It was early the next morning and by now Alex must surely have become concerned enough to want to try and find her.

Jenna's throat was dry and she tried not to think about what she had learned in high school biology lessons. On average a person could survive for only about three to four days without water. She had a way to go yet but no idea whether she would be rescued in time.

Jenna's eyes were accustomed to the darkness now, aided by a small sliver of daylight coming from underneath the door. Hanging above her was an electrical cord attached to a light fitting but there was no bulb. She looked back at that crack of light under the door and an idea came to her.

Frantically she started searching the shelves attached to the brick wall, using her fingers to feel along them looking for something, anything she could use to write a message.

If she could find even a small scrap of paper and a pencil she thought she would be able to slip it through that tiny gap between the bottom of the door and the floor. There was nothing. Jenna let out a small cry of frustration and returned to, her sitting position.

★ ★ ★

Bernie Mitchell and his lawyer sat behind the desk waiting for a response. When the lawyer had requested a face-to-face meeting with the District Attorney he'd initially been fobbed off but when he hinted at what his client had to offer a meeting had been hastily arranged.

Bernie knew the next words that came out of the DA's mouth would decide the course of the rest of his life. While he waited, he reflected on the amazing timing and how close he had come to disaster.

He didn't know how the new information about the Logans' accident had come to light but he did know that it meant his decision to come to the authorities right now was correct.

While Olivia Harris was busy trying to cover her tracks, he was offering her up to her bosses with enough evidence to condemn her to life imprisonment.

The Search is On

Alex hadn't been worried by Jenna's absence at first. He knew Jenna liked her independence and he was pretty sure she would find it irritating if he started phoning her when they'd been apart for more than a few hours. But as it grew dark he started to wonder.

Jenna had no friends in the area other than him and his family. It wasn't as if she could have simply gone to see someone and lost track of the time. He decided to ring his sister.

'Hi, Amber,' he said. 'I don't suppose Jenna has been over at the house today, has she?'

'Not that I know of,' Amber said. 'You haven't had a fight, have you? Is it going to be the shortest engagement in history?' The giggle in her voice told her older brother she was teasing him. 'Let me go and ask if anyone else has seen her.'

'No,' Alex said quickly. He didn't want his whole family thinking he and Jenna had problems. 'I'm sure she'll be home soon, it's fine.'

For half an hour after he ended the call to his sister Alex sat and brooded. He wasn't sure what to do. He had just about made up his mind to call the local police station, despite his doubts about most of the officers' loyalties, when there was a knock at the front door. Jenna must have forgotten her key, he thought, as he went to open it.

'Is Jenna Logan at home?' the man at the door asked. He was dressed in a smart business suit and accompanied by a woman who was dressed just as formally.

'No,' Alex said. 'Who wants to know?' It sounded rude even to himself but the stress of wondering where Jenna had got to had made him snap.

The man produced an identity card. 'Special Agent Jim Collins and

Special Agent Hannah Hart, FBI. May we come in?'

Alex was too stunned to do anything other than move to one side to allow the FBI agents to enter the house. He pulled himself together enough to guide them towards the kitchen and offer coffee.

'We're fine,' Collins said and they all sat at the small table. Alex's thoughts were racing. If Jenna had been in an accident it would have been uniformed police who came to the house. He clung to that thought as he waited for one of the agents to explain what was going on.

'Do you know where Ms Logan is?' Agent Hart asked. Now that they were inside it seemed they had tacitly agreed for her to take the lead. When Alex shook his head she carried on.

'We have reason to believe she may be in danger. I'm sorry to alarm you but it is a very serious situation, linked to an accident several years ago involving Ms Logan's parents.'

'Yes, I know about the accident,' Alex said, 'and Jenna was due to meet someone else from the FBI this morning. Is that connected to it as well?'

The agents exchanged a look.

'It could be,' Agent Hart said.

★   ★   ★

Olivia Harris was half an hour away from getting away with everything she had done. That was all the difference between her walking away from her messed up life with one of the new identities she could have chosen from, and ending up locked in a high security cell.

For ever afterwards she would be haunted by that half hour. If she hadn't spent that time transferring money between various secret bank accounts she could have got away — got away with organising the killings of so many people she had lost count, including Paul and Karen Logan.

Got away with running organised crime rings in several states while being employed at a high level in the FBI.

Got away with kidnapping and planning the murder of Jenna Logan simply because she thought the young woman knew more about her parents' investigations than she'd admitted.

While she was in custody, Olivia expected her right-hand man to arrange for her release on bail. A shame, then, that it was her right-hand man, Bernie Mitchell, who had betrayed her.

★ ★ ★

Jenna was starting to lose hope. Although she'd been in the garage less than 24 hours she was starting to go to pieces and it surprised her. If she'd ever imagined herself in a situation like this — though why would she? — she would have been sure she could have remained calm and come up with something practical to do.

Instead, all she could think about was

why Christina Mitchell hated her so much that she was prepared to let her die a lingering death from dehydration.

She was sure now that it was Christina who was responsible for her predicament and her brain kept focusing on how she would get revenge if she ever got out of the garage alive. It was the only way she could stop herself fantasising about drinking glass after glass of ice-cold water.

When she heard the noise outside she thought at first that she'd imagined it. But no, there it was again. Voices and a crackling noise, like a police radio.

Wishful thinking, she thought, but then there was the unmistakable sound of someone forcing open the lock on the garage door.

Moments later the door was opened and it seemed like she was suddenly surrounded by people. The combination of shock and relief when she saw the police car lights outside made Jenna light-headed and she kept repeating in her head that she must not faint. That would just be pathetic.

For the second time in a week Jenna was taken to hospital by ambulance and Alex joined her within minutes. Just like last time, she was unable to speak to him properly because her voice came out as a croak but she managed to whisper.

'Have they caught her?'

'Who?' Alex said.

'Christina,' Jenna said and Alex realised what she meant.

'Jenna, it wasn't her this time,' Alex said and Jenna's eyes grew wide with disbelief and confusion.

'Who, then?' she asked and then turned to look at the door of her room where two strangers had entered.

'It's quite a long story,' the man said, introducing himself and his colleague. Agent Hart. They gave Jenna a quick summary of what had happened and promised to come back when she was feeling stronger so they could fill in the gaps.

'For now, though,' Agent Collins

said, 'there will be an officer stationed at the door and someone with you at all times, once you leave here, until all the suspects are in custody.'

* * *

Alex sat by Jenna's bed throughout the night. It was likely she would be discharged from the hospital the following day and the way he felt right at that moment he didn't want to leave her side ever again.

Once she had some fluids on board Jenna had felt much better but she was starting to have doubts about staying in Florida.

'Since I've been here my life has been in danger at least three times,' she said. 'New York has this reputation for being a dangerous place to live but this is ridiculous.' She was only half joking.

'Let's talk about it once you're home,' Alex said. He'd always told Jenna he would never want to leave this area but if she decided she couldn't live here he wouldn't hesitate to follow her. They definitely had some serious talking to do before they got married. Alex hoped that once she knew the full story about what had happened it would put her worries to rest.

Time to Say Goodbye

As always, when Christina Mitchell didn't know where to turn she called her father.

'Hi, princess,' he said. 'I was literally just picking up the phone to call you. I need to talk to you about something very serious.'

That snapped Christina out of the despair she'd rapidly sunk into. She'd never heard her dad sound so worried.

'What is it, Dad?' she said.

'I can't tell you over the phone. Listen, pack a bag and I'll send a car over for you. Right now.'

Christina knew better than to argue. If her father said this needed doing then she knew it was true.

She threw some clothes and toiletries into a trolley bag and was outside the hotel within 15 minutes. When she arrived at her father's home, Christina was stunned by the change in his appearance. He looked as if he'd aged several years since she'd last seen him. She ran to him and hugged him.

'Tell me what's going on,' she said and they sat at the dining table while he explained everything. When he'd finished she tried to catch hold of the thoughts that were racing through her mind and sort them into some sort of order.

'If you'd told me this last week I would have said no to what you're suggesting,' Christina said. 'But now . . . it looks like I've lost Alex. And I could be in serious trouble for some of the stuff I've done.'

Bernie raised an eyebrow but she shook her head.

'No, I'm not going to tell you. I should have left it to you. Anyway, it's all in the timing, right? If we're going to be leaving to start new lives, well, count me in.'

Bernie smiled and hugged his daughter as tightly as she had done to him when she arrived. Everything would be OK if they were together. They could start again somewhere nobody knew them.

Bernie had stashed away enough cash over the years to keep them comfortable. Maybe they'd even meet new partners. Maybe find the happy ever after they'd always been looking for.

★ ★ ★

Bernie and Christina Mitchell's happy ever after was going to have to wait for a while. When Bernie's lawyer had finally summoned the courage to tell him the truth about what kind of deal they could expect from the District Attorney, Bernie's reaction veered from anger to disbelief and finally to dejected acceptance.

When they had sat in the DA's office and Bernie had told everything he knew about Olivia Harris he had let himself hope for that slapped wrist he had dreamed he could get away with. But there was no way he could avoid some jail time for the things he'd been involved in over the past 20 years.

At least Christina would be safe and provided for. Bernie's lawyer had managed to negotiate a few days of freedom for Bernie to get his affairs in order. The money he'd stashed away over the years would keep his daughter in comfort while he was away for five years.

And at least they'd managed to agree that he could do his time in relative comfort of a low-security jail rather than the harsh surroundings of the state prison.

Christina was distraught that the offer of new identities had been withdrawn, too. Once she'd come to terms with moving away and starting a new life the advantages of doing so had become clear. A clean slate in a new city — a wealthy young woman would have plenty of opportunities.

She hadn't told Bernie but she planned to change her name once he left. If the authorities wouldn't give her a new identity she'd create her own.

He'd already banned her from visiting him and if she was unable to see the one person who had supported her all her life then she'd have to start relying on herself for the first time.

Instead of being scared at the prospect she was finding it motivational. And she'd made a promise to herself. Never again would she be so blinded by love or jealousy or whatever it had been that made her behave so recklessly towards Jenna Logan.

It was time for father and daughter to say their goodbyes. Christina had promised herself she wouldn't cry but that promise was proving harder to keep than the one about her behaviour.

'Come on, princess,' Bernie said. 'Give me one of your beautiful smiles for me to remember until I see you again.'

'I don't understand why you won't let me visit you,' Christina said for about the tenth time since he'd told her.

'You're supposed to be moving on, making a new life for yourself,' Bernie said. 'I don't want that put on hold for five years because of me.

'Anyway, we can keep in touch. My lawyer says they allow video calls for prisoners whose relatives live far away.'

'I haven't even decided where to go yet,' Christina said. She hadn't been back to her suite at the hotel since Bernie had called and told her to pack a bag.

All the things she'd left behind belonged to her old life and she had access to plenty of money to replace everything once she decided where she wanted to live.

'Well, I know where I'm going and I can't put it off any longer,' Bernie said, giving his daughter a hug and hurrying outside to his lawyer's car. His deal was in jeopardy unless he reported to the prosecutor's office within the next hour.

Christina watched from the window as the car pulled away. Surprisingly the tears of just a few minutes ago had dried up completely. She was Bernie Mitchell's daughter and she was going to face up to her future and stand on her own two feet.

Good News and Bad News

Alex's face was flushed with excitement and he looked as if he might burst if he didn't pass on his news immediately.

'You're not going to believe this,' he said.

'Try me,' Jenna said, amused by his boyish enthusiasm.

'Well, you know Bernie Mitchell's going away for a few years?' They'd both heard the rumours of Bernie's deal with the authorities.

'Yes. And it should be a lot longer,' Jenna said, annoyed now that Alex seemed to be so happy about it. From her point of view it looked like Bernie Mitchell had got off very lightly indeed after all he'd done. She still had a nagging doubt over his supposed innocence regarding her parents' deaths.

Alex tried to regulate his mood but it was impossible.

'Well, listen to this. A lawyer got in touch with Dad today. Seems there's some sort of loophole in the contract he signed when Mitchell took over the hotel.'

'Loophole?' Jenna asked, too curious to carry on dwelling on her earlier thoughts.

'Yes. The lease is going to revert to my parents. And although they don't want to run the place themselves it means there's ready-made jobs for any of my brothers and my sister if they want them.'

At last it seemed like things were looking up for the Shepherd family and Jenna was genuinely thrilled for them. Then something dawned on her.

'Just your brothers and sister? What about you?' she said.

Alex took a deep breath. It was time to share his ambitions for the dive school business. Would Jenna believe in him or laugh? He needn't have worried.

'That's fantastic,' Jenna said after he'd outlined his plans. 'We can stay in this house for a while, then maybe look for somewhere bigger.'

'My thoughts exactly,' Alex said. 'Big enough for our family.'

They kissed and if Jenna was alarmed when she thought about the size of family Alex had come from she didn't show it.

★   ★   ★

That evening there was one of the legendary Shepherd family celebrations. Jenna wondered how her future mother-in-law managed to produce such a feast at short notice and whether she'd ever be able to match up to her as a wife and mother. She was certainly going to give it a very good try.

The main source of amusement at the meal seemed to be testing Jenna on all the Shepherd brothers' names. After going round the table about 20 times she was pretty sure she had them all correct and suspected they were deliberately swapping names to confuse her.

After several champagne toasts to the future of the hotel, Jenna and Alex made their excuses and walked back home.

Since coming home after her kidnap ordeal Jenna wouldn't have thought it possible to feel closer to Alex than on the day he'd proposed but in fact in the days since then she had grown to love him even more.

It was late and they both had busy days ahead of them so, after a quick nightcap of hot chocolates enjoyed on the decking overlooking the beach, they decided to call it a night.

* ★ ★

Next morning Jenna signed on to her Ask Jenna e-mails for the first time in days, dreading how many messages from Nonnie might be waiting for her. Instead, amongst the junk mail and a couple of genuine work emails, there was a message from Shaun. Its contents finally laid to rest the mystery of the Nonnie e-mails.

'Hi, Jenna, I know my last message sounded a bit abrupt and I'm sorry. I've found something out that you need to know. It's about some weird messages that have been sent to your Ask Jenna column. I guess you know what I'm talking about.

'Anyway, I'm sorry if they've upset or disturbed you. The thing is I think I know who has been sending them. Actually, I'm sure I know. Erica's been acting strange since you left — drinking too much and hiding herself away. I asked her what was going on and she confessed a few things.

'She's never been happy since I asked you to move into the apartment. She says she befriended you so you'd trust her and she pushed you into making the proposal that night.

'Then, even after you left, she couldn't stop herself harassing you, even if it was anonymously, and it seems as if she became addicted to the feeling of power it gave her. She knows what she's done, with hacking your computer and so on, is illegal but she asked me to beg you to forgive her.

'I'm sorry again for the actions of my stupid sister and I hope we can go forward as friends. I'm so disgusted at what she's done I've told her to move out. Shaun.'

With all the serious events that had been happening to her and around her, and the revelations from the past, Jenna had put the Nonnie messages on a back burner in her mind.

Once Adam had cleared the malicious software from her laptop and installed high-level security, they had been confident the e-mails would stop.

Adam had told her she would probably never find out who was behind the Nonnie identity which, he had pointed out, was probably just a play on the word Anonymous.

Jenna had almost given up wondering about it. Now here was proof that the person who had deliberately targeted her peace of mind was someone she had once considered a friend.

With hindsight, Jenna could see she had been foolish to think Erica had ever been a genuine friend. The animosity she had shown towards Jenna, who she saw as taking her beloved brother away from her, had never really changed.

As usual, Jenna tried to look for the silver lining in the situation. At least now Shaun was saying he wanted to be friends. After spending two years of their lives together Jenna had been upset by how abrupt he had been in his previous e-mail so she was happier now.

It made Jenna think about other friends she had been neglecting and she reached for her phone, selecting a contact she had added to the new device but now guiltily realised she had neglected for a long time.

'Hi, Tiff,' she said when her friend answered.

To her relief she and her friend fell

back into conversation as easily as if they had spoken every day.

Jenna came off the phone feeling happy that she still had at least one girlfriend. It was a shame Tiffany and her husband wouldn't be able to come down for the wedding — her friend was about to give birth to their first child.

Everyone was moving on with their lives which was exactly how it should be.

Alex thought Jenna should go to the police about what Erica had done.

'Adam has all the evidence of what was on your laptop,' he said. 'Why should she get away with it?'

'I don't know,' Jenna said. 'With everything else that's happened it just doesn't seem important.'

It was true. Jenna wanted to put Erica, Shaun, the proposal and the Ask Jenna messages firmly in the past. Her priority now was looking towards her future with Alex. Now that Christina had left there was nothing to spoil their happiness.

The next few weeks were a blur of wedding arrangements and work — writing for Jenna and business plans for Alex. The dive school at St Pete Beach was thriving already but his dream was to open more of them along the gulf coast.

He'd joined forces with his youngest brother, Adam, the IT genius, who was going to run the organisational side of the business while Alex concentrated on building up a team of instructors to run the schools.

Jenna had finally made the decision she'd been struggling with for weeks. It was time to say goodbye to the Ask Jenna column.

She'd talked to her editor who already had a couple of possible people in mind to replace her. That had taken her aback but her dented ego would just have to cope with it.

She wondered if she would never be able to check her work e-mails without being reminded of Erica and how she had invaded Jenna's privacy and damaged her peace of mind with the Nonnie messages.

Once that decision had been made, Jenna felt as if a huge burden had been lifted from her.

Although she'd always been proud of helping the young people who wrote in, she hadn't realised what a toll the job had taken on her.

It was supposed to be just a part-time job but in reality she had never been able to shake off the problems of the contributors.

At the back of her mind she was always thinking about one problem or another and how to answer them.

And if she was being completely honest with herself, Jenna knew that the time she spent working on the column was also about having an excuse not to concentrate on the kind of writing she should have been doing.

'So much has happened lately you could write a book about it,' Alex had joked one day over breakfast and Jenna surprised him by taking the idea seriously.

'You're right,' she said, 'and that's exactly what I'm going to do.'

Jenna knew she was in a privileged position. Most writers she knew had to fit their writing around full time jobs.

Here she was with no need to work — the investments her uncle had made for her would provide a comfortable income for years to come. If ever the time was right to get started on that dream novel it was now.

The Lady Vanishes

Bernie Mitchell sat in the small room on his wing at the low security prison that was set aside for prisoners to take part in 'video visits' with loved ones who lived too far away to visit in person.

This was the first time he'd had a chance to take advantage of the system he'd agreed with Christina that they would use. He couldn't wait to see her, even if it was only on a laptop screen.

It wasn't as if he had much to tell her — his first few weeks inside had been pretty uneventful and he knew boredom was going to be the hardest thing for him to overcome during his sentence.

But he was looking forward to hearing how Christina was getting on, where she had decided to live for now and any plans she had come up with for the future.

He'd made sure she would have access to the money he'd stashed away over the years so he was sure she'd be OK financially but he was worried about how she would cope without him to support her emotionally and practically.

Bernie checked the time. The session should have started five minutes ago but the screen was still blank. It was up to the visitor to initiate the session and he had no way of trying to start it up himself.

He was just about to go and look for one of the guards to ask if there was a technical problem when someone entered the room.

Without making eye contact, the guard handed Bernie an envelope that had already been opened. All mail prisoners received was vetted before being passed on even in a low security facility like this one.

Bernie stared at Christina's unmistakable handwriting on the letter. His heart sank as he read the enclosed note: 'Goodbye, Daddy.'

★   ★   ★

Jenna and Alex had been called to a meeting with the District Attorney and the two FBI agents who had headed the investigation.

Jenna hoped that after this she would be able to put everything behind her and get on with her life but she wondered if that would ever be the case. With Christina Mitchell still on the run would Jenna ever have peace of mind again?

'She'd be crazy to come back here after what's happened,' Alex had said the previous evening when they were, yet again, discussing it.

'But she is crazy — we know that,' Jenna said. 'And it's easy for everyone else to shrug it off now she's disappeared. But don't forget she almost killed both of us in that car and me again in the sauna.

'And although it wasn't her that had me kidnapped and held prisoner in that garage I really wouldn't have put it past her.'

Both of them were becoming sick and tired of Christina Mitchell dominating their conversations and their lives. Jenna knew she had to try to move on or at least convince Alex that she was trying.

'Listen, why don't we make a pact? After tomorrow's meeting let's put everything that's happened in a box and leave it in the past,' she said.

Alex took her in his arms.

'Well, maybe not everything,' he said, kissing Jenna. 'Apart from the murder attempts and the corrupt government officials, these have been the best weeks of my life.'

They both laughed and Jenna thought, not for the first time, how lucky she was to be with someone who could turn a deadly situation into something they could find humour in.

Now they were sitting at a long table

in a meeting room at the District Attorney's office. Jenna wondered how many deals had been brokered at this table between the prosecutors and criminals who were trying to bargain for a lesser charge or a lower penalty.

The justice system was a mystery to her and one that she had long ago decided would stay that way. Having seen the hours and the effort her parents had put in trying to uphold the rule of law she had never been tempted to follow in their footsteps.

The DA was chairing the meeting and summed everything up in just a few minutes. Olivia Harris was the main target of the FBI agents' investigation and she would be dealt with in their home state of New York.

The organised crime ring she was involved with, whose leaders had conspired with her in the deaths of Paul and Karen Logan, had been infiltrated and agents were working on building cases to prosecute all the top bosses.

The only loose end, as Jenna and

Alex had been discussing last night, was Christina Mitchell. Their hunt for her had been complicated by the deal her father had negotiated but she was still wanted for two counts of attempted murder.

'Bernie Mitchell wasn't aware of those possible charges against Christina,' the DA said. 'We were hoping she'd be traceable if she took advantage of making a video call to her father in prison but of course she's smarter than that. We do have another lead that's about to be followed up, though.'

When they left the building Jenna was feeling slightly happier. She was actually very impressed with the speed of the operation that had smashed the organised crime ring.

Her opinion had only been slightly changed when the DA warned her that clearing a dozen crime bosses from the state would simply make room for others to move in and take their place.

For Jenna, the important thing was that the people who had been involved in her parents' murders would be facing justice at last.

She had spoken to her uncle a few days earlier to make sure he was up to date with what was happening. It was, after all, his family members too who had been killed.

'Yes, the FBI office up here is keeping me informed,' he said. 'Although it's the New York office dealing with it they seem to feel like they lost family members, too.'

Jenna had noticed that in her dealings with Agents Collins and Hart. They took it personally when one of their own was harmed.

Jenna realised now, more than ever, why her parents had been so highly motivated in their jobs. But she still could never have done that work.

Happy the Bride

Jenna woke at first light. This was the day she'd dreamed of all her life. OK, so the people involved, the cast of characters, had swapped and changed over the years but at last her dream wedding day was here.

She gulped down a quick coffee while she dressed in yesterday's clothes. She wanted to go and check that everything was perfect before anyone else showed up.

Chairs were being set out under the voluminous canopy that dominated the space between the hotel and the sea shore. Jenna closed her eyes and pictured herself and Alex hand in hand, exchanging vows and rings.

Jenna wiped a tear from her cheek as she thought of her dad who would have been so proud to walk her down the aisle between these chairs. Her mother would have spent weeks searching for the perfect outfit.

Alex's huge extended family would fill most of the chairs and although they'd welcomed Jenna as one of their own she still felt her parents' absence like a physical pain.

With a sigh Jenna marched towards the hotel office which was being used to coordinate the day.

A quick chat with the staff in there and a wander round the restaurant where places were already set for the reception, finally satisfied Jenna that everything was under control.

She couldn't put it off any longer — time to get herself ready. Alex's sister, Amber, was waiting for her. She was in charge of hair and make-up, something Jenna happily admitted she had no idea about.

An hour later, Jenna, dressed in the simple ivory silk gown she'd finally chosen only a week earlier, stood in front of the mirror.

'Wow, Amber,' she said. 'I hardly

recognise myself.'

'In a good way, I hope.' Amber laughed.

Jenna had thought long and hard about who she could ask to give her away. In the end she'd realised nobody could take her dad's place so she walked towards Alex alone.

The service was over in a flash and the newly-weds were surrounded by family and friends in the restaurant.

One of Alex's brothers — Jenna thought she knew which one but she couldn't swear to it — stood and raised his champagne glass.

'To the happy couple,' he said.

One of the messages read out during the speeches was from Jenna's uncle. He apologised for the family not being there.

Luckily, Alex's family was big enough for both of them. Jenna wouldn't admit that even though she could now remember all his brothers' names she still couldn't always match each name to the right brother.

She hoped she'd be able to do so by the time any children came along. After all, it would be embarrassing if she couldn't refer to their uncles by their names.

After the meal all the guests moved outside where an area next to the beach bar had been converted into a dance floor for the evening.

Alex's brothers had seemed uncharacteristically nervous towards the end of the meal and the newly-weds were about to find out why. Somehow they had managed to rehearse in secret to perform a dance routine that had everyone in fits of laughter.

Then it was time for the happy couple to do their first dance. They had debated for hours over what song to choose. They didn't really have an 'our song' and weren't keen on any recent music.

In the end Jenna had thought back to the songs her parents had loved and shared with her and there was a particular Madonna song from the 80s her mother had always loved. So Alex led Jenna to the dance floor to the strains of 'Crazy For You'.

Neither of them were good dancers so they just shuffled around enjoying the closeness and the good wishes of all their family and Alex's friends. Jenna still didn't feel a part of those friendships but she was determined to work on that.

After a few more dances Jenna whispered in Alex's ear. Her eyes met her husband's gaze and he nodded. He knew what she meant — it was time to tell everyone where they were going on honeymoon.

All Alex's brothers had been winding him up about the fact he had rarely left the state of Florida in his life. Amber was the only one in on the secret and she'd thrown herself enthusiastically into helping Jenna to make all the preparations.

Their car was loaded with suitcases and Amber had been given strict instructions to make sure nobody got too carried away decorating it with 'Just Married' stuff. Alex grabbed the DJ's microphone and asked everyone for some quiet.

'I don't know why this has become such a big deal,' he said, 'but just to let you all know, my wife and I are off to Hawaii. Our flight leaves in four hours.'

There were a few cheers and a lot of back slapping and then Jenna realised it was time to throw her bouquet. She and Amber had practised for days to make sure her new sister-in-law would be the one to catch it. The look on Amber's new boyfriend's face was a picture.

'See you in three weeks,' Alex and Jenna shouted in unison as they drove away from the party.

Secret Hideaway

Christina Mitchell settled back on to the sun lounger and sipped her cocktail. This place was perfect. If she had a twinge of conscience about leaving her father to languish in prison with no contact she certainly wasn't showing it.

Daddy's millions had allowed her to create a new identity and relocate to this little corner of heaven with very little difficulty.

She planned to stay here as long as she could but at the first sign that someone had recognised her Christina would simply move on again to another highly desirable location.

Christina had been involved in the hotel business as long as she could remember, first moving around with her father from place to place and later managing the hotel at St Pete Beach herself.

She had run that hotel successfully and probably was unaware of a major failing that most people around her had noticed. Although she was responsible for the hiring and firing of senior people she hadn't bothered to get to know any of the housekeeping staff, for instance.

Once they had been taken on, they either did their job impeccably or she made their life hell. They were nameless, faceless operatives as far as Christina was concerned.

How unlucky, then, that working at this luxury hotel where she had based herself was an ex-employee of the St Pete hotel, a former chambermaid who had felt so bullied and unappreciated by the manager of that hotel she had left and returned to her home state just a few months earlier.

When she saw on the news that the FBI were searching for Christina Mitchell it took her all of five seconds to decide to call the number on the screen.

Christina took the final sip of her cocktail and debated whether to order another. She took off her sunglasses as she tried to make this difficult decision and it was then that she saw the half dozen officers enter the pool area.

As they led her away she wondered whether prisoners could make video calls to each other. Probably not.

★   ★   ★

Alex filled Jenna's wine glass and then his own. As they clinked glasses they reclined on their sunloungers and gazed out to sea.

'You're a genius,' Alex said to his new wife. 'This is the perfect place for a honeymoon.'

It had taken them a long while to agree on their honeymoon destination. They both wanted time alone together but Alex had his dive school business to think about and Jenna was working on her book.

It was Jenna who came up with the

perfect solution.

'Here's the answer,' she said, her arms stretched out wide indicating the beach at the back of her house. It took Alex a moment to realise what she meant.

'You think we could stay here for that long without my family coming to bother us?' he said.

'They won't know we're here,' Jenna said. She searched her bookshelf for a moment then handed Alex an atlas opened at a map of the USA. 'Here, close your eyes and point to somewhere on this map.'

Alex laughed and did as she'd said. After a false start that would have seen them spending a romantic honeymoon at the bottom of the Grand Canyon, he pointed at Hawaii.

'Perfect,' Jenna said. 'Now all we have to do is tell everyone that's where we're going and we can stay, undisturbed, exactly where we want to be.'

It took them an hour or so to perfect the plan — they would load up their car with empty luggage and drive off in the direction of the airport before returning home once everyone believed they had left.

Neither of them needed to say it but it was what Alex had thought all his life. If you live in paradise why go anywhere else?

We do hope that you have enjoyed reading this large print book.

Did you know that all of our titles are available for purchase?

We publish a wide range of high quality large print books including:
Romances, Mysteries, Classics
General Fiction
Non Fiction and Westerns

Special interest titles available in large print are:
The Little Oxford Dictionary
Music Book, Song Book
Hymn Book, Service Book

Also available from us courtesy of Oxford University Press:
Young Readers' Dictionary
(large print edition)
Young Readers' Thesaurus
(large print edition)

For further information or a free brochure, please contact us at:
Ulverscroft Large Print Books Ltd.,
The Green, Bradgate Road, Anstey,
Leicester, LE7 7FU, England.
Tel: (00 44) **0116 236 4325**
Fax: (00 44) **0116 234 0205**

Other titles in the
Linford Romance Library:

A YEAR IN JAPAN

Patricia Keyson

When ex-librarian Emma announces she's accepted a year-long position to teach English in Japan, the news shocks her grown children. Enjoying single life after half a year of estrangement from her husband Neil, Emma can't wait to embark upon her adventure in three weeks. Then Neil is hospitalised after a car accident, and needs a carer at home while he recovers. Emma is the only one available to help. Three weeks — can Neil make up for lost time before Emma leaves, and will she let him back into her heart?